TOM HANSEN

A MOONLIT TASK

END GATE SERIES BOOK 1

IceBlazer
Entertainment

A Moonlit Task

Have no fear of moving into the unknown.
Simply step out fearlessly.

Pope John Paul II

PROLOGUE

"YOUR FIRST MISTAKE WAS THINKING that an old Asian woman in an herb shop would sell pot to teenagers." Linda Hamada tapped her fingernail on the worn, wooden counter as she studied the two kids. "Your second mistake," she continued, "was allowing the door to close."

The taller of the two boys, pimple-faced and thin, glanced back at the door. His eyes narrowed and he backed a step toward it.

"Go ahead and try." Linda waved lazily. The thin metal bracelets on her arm chimed together in the quiet shop. "But it's not all bad. Now that you're here, I have the opportunity not only to teach you a valuable lesson, but also to help you out."

Linda smirked for a moment then turned and ducked behind the counter.

The smaller goth boy jabbed his friend with a meaty elbow. They both made for the door.

The taller one got to the door first and tried to push it open. The smaller one slammed into him, throwing him into the door. His face left a grease mark on the glass just above the backwards Ye Olde Herb Shoppe painted on the other side.

"It's stuck," the taller one grunted, rubbing his jaw.

The old woman's voice, wafted up from somewhere distant, like she was deep in a cellar instead of just huddled behind a counter. "It's not stuck, silly. I locked it." Linda sprang up from behind the counter. Her long gray braid whipped around to hang over one shoulder as the sound of a small wooden door banged close in the distance. She held out one of her hands; three rings glinted in the low light. "It's magic." She twiddled her fingertips as tiny wisps of smoke rose from them.

The two teens shot nervous glances at each other. "I told you we shouldn't have come in here!" The shorter boy glared at his friend.

Linda pointed at the squat boy in the front. "Shouldn't you be in math tutoring right now, Kevin? What are you going to say to your teacher tomorrow when you fail that test yet again? You know she really cares about you and just wants you to succeed."

Kevin swallowed, an anxious look on his face. He opened his mouth to say something but nothing came out.

"And Jeff." The old woman raised her head up to peer at the taller boy through her bifocals. "Aren't you supposed to be watching your younger sister?

Jeff blanched, the color of his face nearly matching that of his frosted tips.

"It's no matter. What's done is done. But I have your orders ready." She snapped her fingers. Two paper bags appeared on the old wooden counter.

Jeff's lower lip quivered for a moment before he finally spoke. "How did you know our names?"

"Magic, duh." Linda grabbed her braid and tossed it back behind her shoulder. "At least you won't be smoking dope tonight, or whatever you kids call it these days. Now get over here. Don't be shy."

Neither boy moved a muscle.

Linda sighed and put her hands on her hips. "You know I could pick you up where you stand and move you over here if I really wanted."

Kevin huffed and stuck out his chin. "Oh yeah? Maybe we don't wanna." His voice cracked despite the tough-guy persona.

Linda drew in a slow breath, releasing it after a couple seconds. A large truck thundered up Williamson street, its engine noise matching her mood. She looked both boys up and down for a long moment then pursed her lips.

"When I was a young girl, we were taught to be polite when speaking to others, especially our elders. But what should I expect from teenagers who should be home with their families but are instead out wandering around trying to get high?"

Linda clapped her hands. A thunderous roar resonated through the small shop. Jars of herbs and roots rattled on their shelves behind her. Dust on the floor shook with the violence of the concussion, and both boys cringed, picking up alternating feet as they felt the vibrations.

"Now get over here before I turn you both into mice." She thumbed behind her. "I have a cat in the alley who would love to play. I promise she won't hurt you too much."

After glancing at each other, the two teens minced up to the counter.

Linda picked up the first bag and held it out to Jeff. "Rosemary and hyacinth incense, to help with the dreams. Burn half of one stick before bed and keep your door closed to keep in the smoke. The smell will be a little strange at first, but you'll sleep much better."

Jeff wore a calm, confused look on his skinny face. "Thanks, ma'am."

Linda smiled back and gave his hand a squeeze. "You are very welcome, son."

She straightened her back, wringing her ancient hands together to soothe the encroaching arthritis. She gave the other boy an over-the-glasses glance. "Kevin, Kevin, Kevin."

He seemed taken aback. "What? I don't need nothin'."

Linda continued like she hadn't heard him.

"I don't make love potions. They never work the way you think you want them to anyway. But if you like Ashley you need to show her that you're more than just a tough guy. She likes brains, not muscles." Linda shrugged then folded her arms, waiting for a reply.

Jeff turned to his friend. "You like Ashley?"

Kevin, his face turning red, shrank back. "Yeah."

Jeff grinned, a sly look on his long face. "That's cool. She's got huge ..." He glanced at Linda, his eyes going wide at her glare. "I mean, she's real nice."

Despite his beet-red face, Kevin replied. "Yeah, but she'll never give me the time of day."

Linda interjected. "She will if you start taking your grades seriously, and this should help." Linda slid the bag toward him. "Celery seed and Purple Lady-Slipper powder. Brew this up as a tea, four minutes with boiling water, right before doing your homework for the day. Drink it all down as hot as possible as fast as you can tolerate it, leaves and all. It will help with your concentration."

Kevin looked at her, his eyes betraying a look like that of a feral cat wondering if it can take the food from your outstretched hand. He nodded and took the bag.

Linda's expression became serious, as did her voice. "And you kids don't need to be smoking dope. Trust me on this. I lived through the sixties. Give it a few years; the laws are changing. You can smoke all you want when you're older, once your brains have finished developing. But for now, just be kids. Try not to grow up quite yet. Promise me?"

Both boys lowered their heads and spoke to the floor. "Yes ma'am."

Linda beamed. "Well then, you have places to be. Get on out of here. I need to close up." She snapped her fingers and a small click could be heard at the front door to her shop.

Linda watched the boys shuffle out of. A wistful smile spread across her aged and wrinkled face. This is why she agreed to move out here with Anca, to help people with problems they didn't know they had. Sometimes they just needed a little forceful direction.

Jeff and Kevin certainly weren't the first kids, or adults for that matter, to come into her shop hoping that some secret password would cause her to sneakily lock the door and take them to a back room full of grow-lights and cannabis plants as far as the eye can see. But they were good kids.

She missed them already.

She pulled out a rag and wiped down the counters of her shop, clearing away the day's worth of dust and grime that always seemed to accumulate. It was well past her normal closing time.

Linda finished by sweeping the shop and pulling all the remaining money from the register, counting it up and noting it in the ledger.

Attachment flooded her chest. Pride, the good kind, warmed her from the inside out. It had been hard to keep this place running over the last year, hard dealing with Anca and her mood swings. She was proud of the store's success, but more proud of those she'd helped.

Linda paused at the alley door in the back to take one last look over her shop. Smells of the various herbs and reagents mingled together to create a mosaic of earthiness that grounded her in the here and now. This was her home.

Was.

She wasn't sure what it would be after the big fight she'd had last night.

She flipped off the light switch, plunging most of the store into darkness. A single ancient bulb remained, casting just enough yellowed light for her to see into the store from where she stood.

Pulling out her keys to lock up, Linda wrinkled her nose at the musty smell of the alleyway, which pushed away the sweet, earthy notes of her shop.

Something tickled her mind.

She turned around, pushing out her senses to feel for any signs of motion, of life.

Multiple life forces showed up. Two alley cats ignored each other from across the exit to South Few; a wayward pigeon perched on the new high-rise to the south-west, looking down at the scene. A terrified mouse shivered beneath a pile of discarded clothing so filthy that it was hard to tell what it used to be.

But something about the air felt different tonight, something otherworldly.

To her left something hid in the darkness. Linda turned slowly and eased herself down the stoop and around the handrail. She took a cautious step forward, then another one, hesitating each time, feeling all around her in the ever-shifting landscape.

She stopped and bent down. Her hand quavered as she reached behind a small stack of pallets. The baubles and bands on her arm sung their metallic song as they clinked together.

She paused, tasting the heavy air then stooped down into the muck. Something small and furry poked it's black nose out from behind the wood.

"Well hello there, little thing. I won't hurt you."

A tiny mew echoed along the walls of the alley as Linda picked up a shivering kitten. "It's okay." She stroked its dirty, matted fur. "I'm here for you."

She held it at arm's length and gave it a concerned look. "Well, you're an interesting one, aren't you? What are you doing here?"

It meowed again and she rubbed under its chin. "I know, I know."

She felt something else in the alley, another presence. Something terrifying. The feeling was still there. The nerves in her neck fired, cinching up her shoulder muscles.

She looked around but didn't see anything else looming in the shadows. Something about it was … memorable, like mistakes of your past that haunt your dreams.

Linda fit the kitten into the crook of her arm, holding it close to her chest. Her eyes dilated and her stomach knotted, a response to her intensified senses picking up whatever it was in the alley. It had become uncomfortably quiet over the last few moments. Her heart pounded in her chest while a spark flashed in the back of her mind.

She was being hunted.

She thought about turning around, about going back into the shop, but she needed to know. She needed to see with her own eyes.

As she walked across the alley to her car, she winced against the sharp pricks of the kitten's claws digging in to her skin. "There, there. It's okay."

The cat hissed, digging its claws in more. Linda slowed her walking and pulled the kitten closer to her chest, nestling its pint-sized head under her chin.

She reached her car and detached the kitten's tiny claws from her arm, setting it down on the hood. It hissed before running a few steps, its tiny claws clacking on the metal. Then stopped to lick a paw. Its fur stuck out everywhere, its tiny tail straight up in the air.

She began to ground herself, pull in magic from the various baubles she kept around her wrist, preparing to unleash, should the need arise.

There was a flash of orange in the car window. She looked at the reflection and knew what stood behind her.

No. Not you. You aren't supposed to be here. I took precautions. I thought the spell would hold. I need this time to set things straight.

Linda hadn't had time to unlock the secrets of the relic and break the binding. She rubbed her arm in silent contemplation. Despite the chill in the spring air, the alley felt hot, weighed down with apprehension. She swallowed, wishing for water.

"I forgive you, young one." She spoke, her gaze not on the tiny kitten, but on the reflection in the car window. "Your master knows I cannot fight you."

Linda listened to the din of the downtown hum all around her; the buzz enveloped her with white noise.

"The worst part is that you don't know what you are doing, do you? I should have known; I should have recognized the signs. Should have seen it before ..."

Linda eased out a slow, unsteady breath. She focused her mind on a candle flame in her distant memory, something her mother taught her long ago. Hair on the back of her neck and forearms stood at attention, chills ran up and down her extremities. Her left leg twitched, the nerves flashing uncontrollably.

She didn't want to meet its terrifying gaze. Linda raised a shaky hand and wiped a tear from her cheek. Her lip quivered uncontrollably.

"I'm crying." She let out a stifled laugh before catching herself.

She smiled halfheartedly and watched the moonlit drop on her finger disappear into her wrinkled skin.

She turned around to face the threat, finally meeting those terrible eyes.

The yellow slits looked back at her; no pity, no remorse. The slinking creature cast a shadow that consumed the gap between them. Its tail swished behind it. Back and forth, while it watched her from the dark.

"I'm sorry I wasn't there for you. I hope you find peace, P ..." She stopped herself. "I suppose you will go back and be rewarded for this. I do not envy your dreams tonight, but I harbor no ill will."

The beast padded toward her, one slow step at a time. She took half a step back, then another. She ran into something solid, something metal. Her car.

Her purse fell from her shoulder, hitting the ground, contents spilling over the slimy pavement. She groped for the door handle, for something to steady herself on.

Tears poured down her face as the beast drew ever nearer. The smell of rotten meat lingered in the air between them. Despite its size, it made almost no sound as it padded toward her.

As she resigned herself to her fate, she sensed a presence in the distance; another witch close by. She sent out a message, begging for help. Would they listen and respond?

Death comes but once for the righteous.

She would face it head on.

She stood erect, barely taller than the car. Her hand brushed against something in her pocket. It called to her, mocking. It wasn't the right time, the right situation. She thought she had more time to fix this. It might have been able to help her, to help *him*, but it was too late.

She reached in and grabbed the object. Her hand squeezed its hard edges, making small indents in her skin.

She thought about Kevin and Jeff. The tentative hope on their faces as they took their bags filled her heart with love and caring. She hoped they made it home okay.

The beast lunged for her. She didn't flinch.

CHAPTER 1

I T TOOK ONLY A MOMENT for Edna to disappear. Nancy Moon swore under her breath while searching up and down the aisle. *That woman is going to be the death of me.*

"Edna? Where did you go?"

She blew back the gray hair that flew in her face and abandoned the cart in the aisle, heading toward the front of the supermarket. She rounded the corner and scanned the checkout lines. A middle-aged couple stood in line, the woman rooting through a file folder of coupons. The man glanced up at her briefly before hiding back behind his newspaper. He must have seen the frustration on Nancy's face. As she passed, she noticed the headline with the latest news: *Two More Horrific Deaths Baffle Police.*

The recent bizarre deaths were concerning, but Nancy had someone to find.

She turned left, walking past two more aisles and a woman in her forties with kids in tow before catching a glimpse of Edna's red dress, her black, natural curls pulled into a bun.

"I give that girl any chance to bolt and look what she does." Nancy glanced at her watch, noting the time. She didn't want to miss their show. It was a good thing they weren't that far from Edna's apartment.

"What the …" she mumbled to herself. "Are those college boys?" Edna rarely dated in her age-bracket.

She set her jaw and strode up the aisle toward the three boys and Edna.

She cleared her throat and folded her arms. "What do you think you are doing, young lady?"

Edna had a hand on one of the boy's biceps. Her coffee-color skin was a stark contrast to the boy's pale-pink arms.

Nancy cleared her throat again, intensifying her glare.

Edna finally turned around. Red lipstick glistened on her big, dopey grin while her dark brown eyes glinted guiltily in the store's overhead lighting. Wrinkles that she insisted didn't exist gave her true age away, especially standing next to young men like she was.

"We were just talking."

"Talking?" Nancy could feel her blood pressure rising. "These *boys*"—she nodded with a curt smile at the one closest to her—"are in their twenties."

Edna sighed, annoyance pouring from her tone. "I know that, *Mom*."

The sarcasm in Edna's voice irritated Nancy, but there were better ways to deal with her aged friend's impertinence. Nancy decided on a humiliation tactic this time.

Nancy's eyes narrowed. She reached out and grabbed Edna's hand, extricating her from the young man.

"I'm sorry, but I need to get her back to the old-folks' home; she is always wandering out." Nancy gave a curt nod to the confused young man before she started back up the aisle, Edna in tow.

"Why do you always have to harsh my buzz?"

"Do you even know what that means?" Nancy tried to control the eye-roll that her mind begged her to perform.

"I was trying to get a date." Edna spurted out, huffing while being nearly dragged up the aisle.

"With college-age boys?"

"Well yeah, who else?"

Nancy stuck a bony finger in Edna's direction. "You are three times the age of those boys!"

Edna grinned mischievously. "I know! Isn't it delicious? If you hadn't come and taken me away, I might've had a chance with one of them."

Nancy let out a restrained breath. "Do you even know what time it is? *Dancing with the Stars* starts in twenty minutes and we are still out shopping."

Edna cocked her head to the side, revealing her gray roots. "Don't worry, we have time. Besides, it's being recorded back at my place."

Nancy felt the vein in her left temple pulse and took a long breath to calm herself. She tried to think of happy things. "If I have to miss it again this week because you can't keep your skirt on, I swear ..."

Edna grabbed Nancy in a bear hug. "Nancy, I say this as your younger, very hot friend. You need a man."

Exasperated, Nancy extricated herself from the hug. "We're not having this conversation now. Besides, I thought you were enjoying being a widow. Thelma and Louise, remember? Now let's go get some wine to celebrate not having the toilet seats left up in our houses."

She headed back around the corner to look for her cart.

Edna snickered and she ran to catch up as Nancy turned down the coffee aisle.

Nancy closed her eyes and pulled in a long, deep breath, holding it in for a three-count before letting it out. She savored the deep aromas of the various coffee blends and the sumptuous flavors begging to be released into the next cup.

"I could move here. Pitch a tent and just live right in this aisle."

Edna bent down and squinted at the bag of pre-ground store-brand coffee. "I could have had my own tent pitched tonight if you would have just let me have a few more minutes," she mumbled.

Nancy couldn't help her smile, but still tried to cover it up by slapping Edna's head with the small notepad for her grocery list. "If I'm the one that needs a husband, then what was that cradle-robbing stunt you just pulled? "

Edna scoffed. "I never said you need a husband. I said you need a man. A real one, in your bed, between your legs. It's been too long since Richard disappeared."

Nancy felt blood rush to her head. She grabbed the nearest box of tea and tried to look like she was studying it with great vigor. She didn't want to think about her husband just up and disappearing on her a couple days before her fifty-eighth birthday. It was still too soon to worry about a long-term relationship. Even after four years, the police wouldn't declare him dead, only missing.

"You know it's not easy for a woman my age."

"And what age is that?" Edna gave Nancy the look again, crossing her chubby arms.

"Oh you can't start with me on that. You're younger than me."

"Only by three years."

Edna had to almost jog to catch up. "I love it when we fight; make-up sex is just so much better."

Nancy felt her face flush. "You're incorrigible. Children might hear you."

"Psh. Nothing children don't talk about on the playground anyway."

Nancy groaned inwardly while still smiling outwardly. They arrived at the wine aisle. Nancy parked the cart at the end and walked past the white wines, holding her list in her hand.

"Okay, we need a dark red for next weekend, and I prefer something lighter for reading."

Edna reached down for one of the large jug-style gallons of wine on the bottom shelf. "Now isn't this a good deal?"

Nancy put her hands on her hips. "Edna Maddox, you're just trying to push my buttons, aren't you?"

Edna shrugged sheepishly, reminding Nancy of a naughty, scolded child. "Too on the nose?"

Nancy grinned and nodded her head. She held up her fingers a quarter-inch apart. "Only a little."

"You're right, we're two old ladies. Well, one of us is, anyway." She winked at her best friend. "And life is too damn short for bad wine. Besides, now that you and I are both officially unemployed, we need to start planning trips." Edna put back the jug of cheap wine.

"Oh no." Nancy waggled a bony finger at her friend. "I think we need a cooling off period from the last road trip we took. Besides, it wasn't exactly my choice to take early retirement. It was either that or get laid off. I might still go find myself a new job."

"Oh, but you can't! We've had so much fun these last couple months."

She had to admit the time since she'd quit had been fun, but she still worried about paying for bills and ensuring she was setup for retirement. Her husband's gothic home, long-owned through the family, was certainly a boon, but it was old, creaky, and in need of a lot of maintenance, and that cost money, something Edna didn't have to worry about.

Edna walked around the aisle and disappeared out of view while Nancy looked across the wide selection of red wines. She loved Cabernet and Shiraz, but lately she had been looking for something … unique.

An odd-looking bottle caught her attention. While most of the bottles had round bases, this one was square, with a deep purple glass. The exterior seemed to be covered in a layer of dust but closer inspection showed it to be frosted stippling. The etched lines cascaded across the bottle, dipping underneath the label and back out the other side. It reminded her of the sea. She pulled it off the shelf, noting it was the only one of its kind. She was surprised by its heft, like the liquid inside was made of more than just fermented grape juice.

Two layers of wax, a deep crimson topped by a milky-translucent white, sealed the top and dripped halfway down the neck. She turned it over in her hands, eyeing the beautiful scrollwork.

"That's some kind of Asian language?" Edna looked over her shoulder then held up two bottles for Nancy's approval. Upon securing the nod, Edna placed them in the cart.

"Chinese maybe?"

The glass felt cool and the dark liquid inside called to her, creating a yearning she couldn't describe. She paused and gently turned the bottle on its side to look at the bottom. As some part of her mind expected, there were more of these rune-like characters etched into the bottom of the glass, but no, these were not the same. She couldn't really put her finger on it but they felt ... different.

Despite the desire to keep it, Nancy moved to put the bottle back.

"What are you doing?" Edna stood to her side, her hands on her hips.

"I was going to put it ..."

Edna grabbed it from Nancy and put it in the cart. The thick liquid inside sloshed with the sudden motion. "How many times do I need to force you to try new things, huh? Get out of your house once in a while. Live a little."

Nancy smiled halfheartedly as she stood up. Despite their differences, Nancy valued Edna's friendship. The two had been through a lot.

She felt a bit of a loss as she watched it head down the aisle with Edna pushing the cart.

Edna stopped and turned around, a look of annoyance on her face. "Well, we going or what?"

Nancy turned onto Edna's street. Right outside the entrance to Edna's posh renovated loft was a large moving van. Two men and a woman were hefting a couch into the front door. The lamplight overhead cast elongated shadows into the street. Why were people moving in this late at night?

"Now how am I supposed to get in?" She glanced down at the time. Three minutes until the show started. They were pushing it as it was, and now the moving van blocked the entrance to the underground parking lot.

"Just pull up in front of the alley. We can move the car after the show." Edna pointed to the alley a dozen feet ahead of the moving van.

Nancy hesitated for a moment, pondering the legality and the sensibility of leaving in front of an alley before finally going for it, parking and turning off the car.

As soon as her hand left the dangling keys, an overwhelming feeling washed over her, like someone whispering directly into her head. "I need to go down the alleyway." Her own words surprised her, as they sounded otherworldly, like someone had taken control of her voice for a moment.

Edna looked at her quizzically. "What are you talking about?"

Nancy tried to shake the intrusive feeling that had come and gone. "Sorry ... I don't know, I just had a sudden desire to go down the alleyway."

Edna narrowed her eyes, leaning forward a bit. "Is this related to your dreams? You refuse to tell me what the woman keeps saying to you every night. Are those still going on because if they are I know someone ..."

She trailed off as she looked at Nancy's eyes wide with shock.

A small squeak escaped Nancy's lips.

"What's ..."

Something large, orange, and heavy slammed into the passenger door, hurling Edna toward the middle of the car. Nancy's heart raced. The back of her hand hit the steering wheel. Pain shot up her arm. She tasted blood in her mouth.

The large shape jumped onto the hood of Nancy's car, cutting off the lamplight streaming in through the windshield.

It was a gigantic cat with large, dark stripes across it's back. The weight of the massive feline lurched the car downward, stressing the shock absorbers. Streetlights cast oddly beautiful wave-like shadows on the hood of her car. Its tail swished back and forth in graceful but jerky, agitated strokes.

Edna sneezed, then hiccuped.

Nancy gasped. What the hell was a tiger doing in downtown Madison, Wisconsin? Her mind raced, trying to make sense of the situation. "Oh, God!" She remembered the headline on the newspaper: the vicious deaths of late. A shudder ran up her spine, but she set her jaw. She wasn't going to be the next victim.

The large cat looked at both women for a long moment then opened its mouth and bared its teeth before lifting its paw to its mouth to lick.

"Lock your door." Nancy's could barely hear her own voice over her thundering heart.

Both women locked their doors. The cat eyed Nancy. Her heart froze. Something deep inside her chest tugged, like a distant memory trying to rise to the surface. *You have nothing to worry about.* Nancy shuddered again.

The large cat turned away, continuing to groom itself.

Edna craned her head up an inch to look at the cat. "We should call someone."

Nancy nodded, slowly. "Yes, please do." Her voice was distant, methodical.

"My purse is in the backseat."

"Can you reach it?" Nancy didn't dare take her eyes off the beast.

Edna rooted around with an arm behind her, trying to reach her purse in the backseat while keeping her face forward. "I don't think so. Can you honk?"

Nancy pursed her lips, thinking through her options. Suddenly she came upon an idea. She turned the key a click, grabbed the turn signal, and twisted.

The wipers sprang into action, squeaking along the outside of the windshield. A half second later, the sprayers kicked in, wiper fluid spewing all over the glass.

The cat looked up again and bared its teeth at the women. With a swish of its tail and a squeak of the shocks, it jumped off into the street and bounded through Central Park before disappearing into the night.

Nancy and Edna sat in silence for a while, the elevated breathing between them eventually calming down.

When they dared a glance at each other, Edna was the first one to lose composure. She roared with laughter. Nancy followed immediately after.

They settled down after a minute of nerve-calming hysterics and, after a careful look around the car to ensure the cat was truly gone, dared venture out. Nancy stood watch while Edna reached into the backseat to get at her cell phone. That was when Nancy heard the moan from the alleyway.

CHAPTER 2

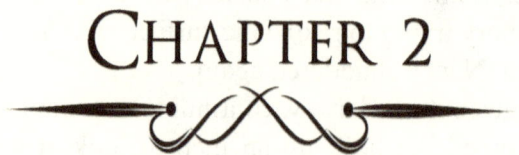

"I THINK WE NEED AN AMBULANCE!"

"What?"

Nancy pointed as she walked past the hood of her car. There on the white hood, pooling in the furrows of the dents and scrapes from the beast's claw marks, was blood glistening a sickly red in the streetlight. She took a couple steps past the sidewalk and stopped at the entrance to the alley. Her stomach tensed and she reflexively pulled her hand to her middle.

The air hitting her face was warm and musty, like a swamp. Appliances dumped their steamy air into the alley and filled the background with an eerie hum.

There was something else, a presence. Despite the din of the alley, Nancy could feel it, like a tugging on her heart, calling her. She couldn't ignore it.

"I think I heard something."

Edna nervously scanned around. "What are you talking about? Did the cat come back?"

Nancy took a hesitant step into the alley. What was she doing? This wasn't her. The most adventurous thing she did on a Monday night was watch television. Her most wild nights involved an entire bottle of wine and her best friend laughing, or maybe a good book. She couldn't get the notion that a tiger was loose on the streets of her hometown out of her head. The gruesome deaths in the news suddenly made sense and she wondered why no one had mentioned that it was a loose tiger.

"You're not going in there." Edna screeched, her voice raising an octave. "There could be another one of those … things in there!"

"I'll be fine. Just call 911." Nancy couldn't quite put her finger on it, but there was no anger in the alley. Only pain. Something in her gut told her the tiger was gone, no longer a threat. She needed to find the source of that pain.

"Oh no, if you're going to get yourself killed, I'm not going to stand here chitchatting on the phone."

Nancy took another step before Edna's arm looped in hers, concern wore Edna's expression and Nancy smiled back grimly. "I'm fine. I just want to look. Morbid curiosity?"

It seemed to satisfy Edna, but Nancy knew it was more than that. There was something waiting for her around the corner. She was being pulled to this. Someone called her into the darkness.

The walls enclosed them as the hum grew louder.

Nancy got to the corner and turned.

The alley opened onto a perpendicular street, lined with the back doors of dozens of shops. A white 1962 Chevy Malibu was parked just inside the alley. Nancy recognized the car as one her father had lusted over when she was a teenager. Lamplight streamed in the other side, illuminating the car and the grisly scene before it.

A body lay crumpled against the driver's side of the car, slumped over at an acute angle on the ground. Dark red splotches marred the white paint job of the old sedan. Nancy had the foreboding feeling that more blood lay on the ground, disguised in the muck and shadows.

Edna let out an audible gasp. Nancy's stomach lurched, spewing a little bit of bile into her throat. She swallowed it down, along with a disgustingly sweet copper taste in her mouth. She wanted to turn and run, but she felt compelled to investigate. She shuddered, thinking about her dreams since Richard had left. There were too many similarities. She shoved the thoughts out of her head.

"Hurry Edna."

Edna nodded, eyes wide at the scene before them. "I'll wait for them at the street."

Edna dialed while Nancy turned back to the scene. Again, she wondered what she was doing. Why was she the one investigating when Edna was the adventurous one? She fought to keep the growing sense of loneliness at bay. She was exposed, and every shadow seemed to conceal a threat.

Something rustled to the side of her. Nancy jumped, startling herself with how on edge she was.

A tiny kitten mewed at her as it took a step out of the shadow. Its fur was matted and dirty, obscuring the white and black spots. It was barely taller than her ankle, and seemed too emaciated to be able to stand. It paused and shook something off its paw.

"Dear heavens!" Nancy clutched her chest with her hand, feeling the thumping of her heart. "You scared me to death. What are you doing here, little one?"

Nancy bent down to touch the cat but stopped before getting too close. Its little tail shook as it mewed again.

"I can't do anything for you right now. You'll have to wait."

Nancy took a few more steps toward the woman. The kitten followed behind her.

The silence was terrifying. Nancy had to say something to keep her mind from going to darker places.

"Your big cousin was a naughty kitty." Nancy shivered.

She stepped closer toward the grisly scene.

Oh dear.

The sight was bad enough, but the smell was horrifying. Nancy gagged, resisting the overwhelming urge to throw up.

She could only see the profile of the victim. She was Asian, or at least the parts of her that were recognizable were. Her blouse was shredded and she had a huge gash across her torso. The tattered remains of her clothes were scattered around her. A purse lay on its side, the contents strewn out across the pavement. Gashes in the car's paint marked near misses from the beast.

"You poor thing. I'm sorry it ended this way."

The woman's chest did not rise or fall. Nancy let out a breath she didn't realize she was holding. Her mind assessed the situation, checking off details. Brutal death, blood everywhere. Should she check for a pulse? Her consideration was cut short when something brushed across her ankle. Nancy glanced down at the kitten.

The kitten hissed, its fur bristling.

"You came. I was worried you didn't hear me," said a scratchy voice from the darkness.

The voice sent Nancy's heart racing. She looked up and saw the woman's head had turned to look at her.

Half of her face was shredded and raw, like someone had taken a cheese grater to her skin. The whole scene looked like the grim remains of a torture horror movie, one of Edna's guilty pleasures.

Nancy's nerves fired all at once. She froze and shook at the same time, unable to move. Tingles shot up and down her body along with a feeling of déjà vu. She fought the urge to throw up.

"Please, come." The woman's arm moved.

Nancy rushed to the woman's side, kneeling down on the alley floor, all pretense of staying clean gone as she realized this woman was still alive.

"I'm here. I'm here." Tears welled in her eyes as she looked at this woman. The body was so torn, Nancy didn't know where to put her hands.

"You heard my call. I need your assistance, Moon Called." The woman trailed off. Her one undamaged eye glazed over and rolled back in her head.

The woman coughed, blood spattering from her mouth in an arc through the dim light. Some of it landed on Nancy's face and blouse. The woman's one un-maimed eye looked at her again, recognition on her damaged face.

Relief flooded Nancy's mind. She leaned in closer to hear the quiet words of this dying woman. She hoped Edna had made the call. She tried to ignore the gore and focus on the fact that the woman was still alive somehow.

"My name … is Linda." The woman coughed again. "Linda Hamada. I run the herb shop." Her shredded hand raised to indicate the building next to the car.

"Hello, Linda. My name is Nancy. Nancy Moon. Help is on the way. My friend is calling an ambulance."

The woman smiled, or tried to with what remained of her face.

"You are latent." Linda sounded almost surprised at her own statement.

"Latent?"

Linda tried to smile, but her grotesque features looked horrific. "I'm sorry I called you. I thought you … you have much to learn, Nancy of the Two Moons. I only wish I had time to teach you." She paused to try to breathe, a gurgling sound in her chest as it rose and fell. "You are a witch, and I need your help." She devolved into a coughing fit with these latest words. More blood oozed out of her wounds with each shake of her frail body.

Nancy smiled, emotion finally releasing along with a flood of tears.

Please don't die. Not here. Not like this.

Linda wasn't making much sense, but Nancy didn't expect her to. The woman was on her deathbed. Nancy was only there to comfort her.

"Please, take."

Linda paused to take a breath. After a moment, the dying woman's hand rose into the air and made its way slowly to Nancy. It shook violently. Nancy reached out and took the hand in hers. Her skin was cold and thin. She noticed the woman's other hand was bloodied and torn, lying limp to the side. What remained of that hand twitched in an eerie staccato rhythm.

Nancy pulled her gaze back to the woman's face, trying to forget the image of that twitching hand.

"You must find Peter!" The woman's voice held an urgency to it that caught Nancy off guard.

"I'm sorry, I don't know what you mean, Linda. Who is Peter?"

"He needs help. He is trapped and this will help him, but not until he is ready. I do not know how to unlock it. I only retrieved it … Anca …" She paused to catch her breath.

The woman's hand continued to tremble. Nancy finally realized Linda was trying to give her something. She carefully opened the dying woman's hand and let the object slip into her palm. It was cold, dark, heavy, and covered in sticky blood. The light bouncing off its smooth surface looked green in the darkness of the alley.

Echoes of an emergency vehicle worked their way through the chilly night air and down between the old buildings, into her ears. She was unable to pinpoint their direction.

"Please, Nancy, tell him he is forgiven. It is not his fault. Witches are dying. Promise me—"

Nancy leaned back as Linda devolved into series of wracking coughs. A horrifying wheeze rattled in her throat, and pink foam bubbled out of her mouth.

"You need to save your strength."

Linda shook her head, coughing again, then finally getting control. Her voice was tiny, barely a whisper and each phrase was a struggle. Nancy had to lean in close to even hear, her ear an inch from the dying woman's bloodless lips. "This is your task … set things right … I will be close … tied to you … Nancy of the two …"

Linda's face contorted with pain or fear. Nancy wasn't sure which.

Panic rose in Nancy's chest again. "No! Don't go. The ambulance is here!"

Nancy pulled Linda's hand to her lips and kissed it. The woman's good eye lolled back in its socket.

She was still.

Tears erupted from Nancy's eyes as the gravity of the situation hit her. This woman had died in her arms. In her brief care.

"I … will find him. I will find Peter. I promise." The words poured out of Nancy and she didn't know why. She had no idea who Peter was or how she would find him, but she didn't regret her promise, not in this dark time. What else do you say to someone dying in your arms? Who was Peter? Who was Anca? What was going on? None of that mattered now.

The sirens grew significantly louder, localizing behind her.

Nancy heard the screech of brakes as the siren came to a full stop. Sounds of footsteps and slamming doors echoed down the narrow alley.

She heard voices in the distance, but they were too hard to pinpoint, and none of them made sense. Unintelligible. She turned to look for the help Linda needed.

The sensation of someone else in the alley caught her attention, like a feeling of motion just outside her purview. She turned back, expecting Linda to be trying to move again, but the woman lay motionless. Her one seeing eye glazed and her battered hand sat limp. It didn't twitch. Neither did her chest rise again.

Despite the blood and torn flesh, Linda looked more at peace.

"Peter. Anca." Nancy spoke the names aloud, surprising herself with the steadfastness of her voice. A solitary tear broke from her eye and traveled down her cheek before landing on her arm.

"I'm so sorry, Linda." She looked the torn body one last time. The old woman's skin was pale in the moonlight, nearly translucent, her life essence pooled about her in the muck and dark. She was a figment of what she once was, an apparition to haunt Nancy for the rest of her days.

Something blue and shiny flashed and she looked up, only to have the image disappear from her mind. It was all too much for her; her mind had started playing tricks. She was already seeing ghosts.

Just before the paramedic grabbed her around the shoulders to gently direct her away from the grisly scene, Nancy slipped the object she palmed into her coat pocket.

The dirty kitten's tiny claws made terrifying screeches on the paint as it tried to gain traction on the hood of Nancy's car.

After the last two hours of her life, the noise was music to Nancy's ears. It grounded her in a morose reality, and kept her mind from wandering back down the dark alley where Linda's body lay covered with a blooded sheet.

She stretched, putting her hands high up into the air as she tried to get the knot out of her back. The object Linda had given to her dug into her side slightly, reminding her of its existence.

"Let's go over your story one last time, shall we, ma'am?"

Officer Brown, according to his nametag, held his notebook and pen at the ready. His eyes were wide in anticipation of her story.

Nancy nodded, her thoughts drifting back to the poor woman in the alley.

"Officer."

"Yes?"

She turned back to him almost in a daze. "Did you ever figure out what happened?"

He had been the first one to throw up upon reaching the alleyway, though she suspected it wouldn't be a good idea to bring that up now. She was amazed she hadn't done the same. The whole situation was obscene.

The officer glanced at his notes. "As far as we can tell, it happened just like you said. We found tufts of orange fur embedded in her wounds and in the scrapes of not only her car but yours as well."

Nancy nodded. But the whole thing didn't add up. "She told me about Anca. Did you contact them already?"

"Oh yes, her partner, Anca"—he flipped back one page of his notepad—"Petran."

Nancy glanced over at Edna, twenty feet away, sitting in the back of the second ambulance to arrive. She was munching on some pretzels. Nancy suddenly realized how hungry and tired she was.

"Ma'am?"

Nancy ached for sleep. Her lower back twinged shooting pains down her leg, and she couldn't avoid the tangy taste of copper in her mouth. Her hand wouldn't stop trembling and she felt like she should simultaneously scream and cry.

She was tired, sore, dirty, covered in another person's blood, and nearing the end of her patience. She loved the public servants, but this was getting out of hand. Did it really take three people to take her statement? Did they not have at least the decency of offering her coffee or a place to sit?

Worst of all, they hadn't even let her talk to Edna.

Nancy trailed her fingernail over one of the claw marks in the hood of her car, her thoughts wandering.

She cackled. She didn't even care that she was laughing like a crazy woman.

Officer Brown looked at her questioningly.

"My insurance company is going to love me," she said.

Nancy fingered the small, smooth object in her pocket. The blood had long since dried on it. She felt guilty not divulging the item to the detectives, but something about the earnestness in the woman's eyes—it was definitely her eyes—made Nancy hold back.

Don't give it to the police; this is your task, they had said to her. She wondered if this was how Frodo had felt.

"Ma'am?"

Nancy stood up, squaring her shoulders and looking the young man in the eye. "Look, I'm sure you have a job to do, but I've already told my side of the story twice, to Detectives Grady and Ankler over there. They have all the information, if you could just check with them."

She glanced back into the alleyway at the flashing lights from the police cameras then turned back to the officer.

"I just want to talk to my friend, make sure she's okay. I haven't been allowed to talk to her for well over an hour, and quite honestly, I'm going to throw up pretty soon if I have to sit in these bloody clothes any longer." She crossed her arms in front of her and gave him the teacher-knows-you're-lying look she'd perfected in her twenty years at Madison Elementary. May I go?"

Officer Brown opened his mouth then snapped it shut. He nodded. "We'll contact you if we have any other questions."

"Thank you." She picked up the small kitten and strode toward her friend.

"How is Officer McNaughty over there?" Edna had a twinkle in her eye despite the grim situation. She glanced down at the kitten and took a step back.

"Officer Brown, and I'm pretty sure I changed his diapers at one point, so don't go getting any ideas."

Edna offered the small bag to Nancy, who grabbed a handful of pretzels at the behest of her rumbling tummy. She didn't realize how hungry she was until the first crunchy pretzel was in her mouth. They tasted like a five-star meal all by themselves. "You get the third degree too?"

"Oh yeah, the Bobbsey Twins Investigator Unit is quite impressive." Nancy grabbed a couple more pretzels and popped them in her mouth. She turned to watch the investigators conferring with the officer. Nancy wasn't going to talk to them again until she got some sleep.

Sleep.

The thought made her nervous. What dreams would haunt her tonight?

"I got the guest bedroom all made up for you."

Nancy finished munching and swallowing her snack before responding. "Thanks, but I really want to go home. I just want my bed tonight. I could use a couple garbage bags so I don't get anything in my car, or a change of clothes."

Edna nodded. "I understand. Anything to keep you from being in one of your moods."

"One of my moods?"

Edna flashed a smile and a small wink. "Of course. I'm just waiting to hear all about how miserable your life is now that you missed *Dancing with the Stars* two weeks in a row."

CHAPTER 3

T HE DOORBELL CHIME HAD NOT yet faded when Nancy opened her eyes. Daylight streamed through the second-story bedroom window of her century-old gothic home as the haze of sleep sloughed off her mind. She blinked once then bolted upright when the doorbell rang a second time. Pains coursed through her back as she sat up too fast. She winced and put her hand on her lower back for support. Glancing at her nightstand, her eyes went wide at the time.

"Ten o'clock!"

Ignoring the scream in her back, Nancy hurried to throw on a robe and shuffled out. She held onto the handrail, taking each step carefully, counting them down in her head from twenty. The doorbell rang again as soon as her foot hit the landing.

"I'm coming. Hold your horses."

She glanced in the mirror beside the door, not pleased with the banshee that stared back. She'd amazed herself last night by staying awake long enough to shower, though she did fall asleep before she was able to change from a towel to real clothes.

Linda's blood. The memory caused a shiver to go down her spine. She pushed it out of her mind.

She smoothed back her unruly hair, pulled her robe closed, and opened the door.

Bright sunlight streamed around a small figure in the doorway.

"Hello?" Nancy couldn't make out a face through the overbearing sunlight.

"Miss Moon?"

The tiny high-pitched voice was instantly recognizable. "Billie. I'm sorry. I was sleeping in and didn't hear the doorbell. What's up?"

Billy Piper's mother had pulled him out this year to homeschool him. He spent his days earning money by doing odd jobs while other children his age were busy in school.

"Uh yeah, so I was trying to collect for the paper from Mrs. Valanor," Billy said, turning and pointing across the street at the house opposite hers, "but no one is answering. Do you know if she's on vacation?"

Shielding her eyes against the glaring sunlight, she looked at the house, noting the sagging roofline on one side. Billy was a sweet kid, but failed to notice things right in front of his face, like the six-foot tall 'for sale' sign in the front yard. "Mrs. Valanor passed away about two months ago, Billy. Did you not hear? They are trying to get the house sold."

"Oh, um, I didn't realize that. I thought someone else was mowing her lawn, though, when I came by. Well, thanks, Miss. M."

Billy spun and ran back down her driveway. He hopped on his bike lying on the side of the road, and took off.

Nancy stepped out onto the sidewalk, keeping a hand over her eyes. She normally woke up before the sun and felt uneasy being in her bathrobe this late in the day.

Gertrude Valanor had been quite the collector, as she called herself, but Nancy knew better. It had been a compulsion, and the house was filled to the brim with junk.

Nick, Gertrude's son, was a nice man, overworked with three teenagers, and living in Florida. It was too much for him to be up here personally to take care of his mother's things, and as such had hired a company to sell off the property.

Despite the sagging roofline, the yard was well-maintained and the broken window in the front had been fixed. The sign had been posted the day after the funeral, but Nancy had never seen anyone come by to look, even after companies had cleared out all the junk. It had taken the crew three days and twice as many trucks.

Something looked different with the front yard, though, and Nancy realized it was the sign. There was a bright red SOLD plaque hanging from a yellowing chain underneath the realtor's name. It swung in the breeze, the hint of a squeak barely making it to Nancy's ears.

She wondered who her new neighbors would be. She hoped it was a younger family, with kids. Too many people on this street were like her: alone, single, widows and widowers.

Single. It was a derogatory term at her age. Thoughts of her long-time husband flooded her mind, but she pushed them out. He had done enough damage to her already by up and leaving four years prior. It had taken countless therapy sessions and a trip to a loss retreat for her to finally get over him leaving her. That was where she had met Edna, and her life had taken on renewed vigor.

Remembering her friend brought forth the events of the previous evening. She turned and headed back inside. She needed to call Edna, but first, she wanted to take a look at the object Linda had given her.

By the time she had gotten home the night before it had been nearly midnight, and for a woman who was normally in bed by nine, that was no small feat.

Still the dreams had come, as they had since Richard left. Someone calling out her name, unseen. More a shadow than a person, always out of reach. Hints of blue and white, ruffles, and the scrape of bare feet on wood floor just out of sight around a corner as she turned her head this way and that.

They didn't come every night, but often enough that it was a common occurrence. Edna thought it was ghosts trying to contact her. Nancy thought it was just her mind trying to process Richard's disappearance.

Last night's nightmare contained no blue dress, no woman with a singsong voice. This time it was the black tip of a tail and the ever-present crying of an aged Asian woman.

She got some coffee brewing and retrieved her bloody coat from the laundry room to bring the item back to the kitchen.

The object inside the pocket was cold to the touch and caked with dried blood. She cringed as she rolled it around in her fingers, the coppery sick taste seemingly transferred through her fingertips.

It was a tiger, sitting on its haunches, looking proud and regal. Its mouth hung open in a growl as it stared straight ahead with piercing eyes. Its thick head borne by broad, powerful shoulders.

She stepped up to the sink, turned on the hot water and scrubbed off the dried blood with yesterday's washcloth.

Underneath was an intense deep green of stone that revealed itself as she kept scrubbing. The stone was slightly translucent. She'd seen jade before, but she didn't remember the colors being quite this intense. The glossy stone emanated sophistication, a stateliness mirrored in its feline figure.

She felt something toward this object; it was hard to pinpoint, like the bottle of wine she found the last night. There was a memory trying to surface, though she was sure she had never seen anything similar to this before.

It reminded her of the treasured egg her mother had kept on the mantle, a family heirloom passed down through generations. She remembered the scolding her mother had given her when she had dragged a chair over to get a closer look.

This jade figurine was almost … sacred. It belonged to someone. It had a history.

Once she was done, she placed it on her butcher-block countertop and observed it from afar while pouring coffee for herself.

It was about three inches tall, with a half-inch thick base as long and as wide as the cat that sat upon it. The tiger's head was up, alert, its eyes focused straight ahead. She could almost imagine the tip of its tail tapping the ground beside its feet, a steady thump of grandeur and poise. Her memory plucked at the previous night's string, reminding her of the correlation between the figure on her countertop and the one that left scratch marks on her car.

But there was something more, a tug on a memory that had taken place even earlier. Maybe it was the sip of coffee, but an idea had been percolating.

After picking it up, sure enough, she found some strange looking chicken scratch under the base that looked vaguely familiar yet otherworldly.

She placed it down on the counter again, taking a step back. Why a tiger figurine? Why was Linda holding this after being mauled by the same? Was it some calling card for a tiger murderer? Did Linda know her killer?

That's when the phone rang. Edna was right on cue.

"Well, will you look at that." Nancy looked out her kitchen's window. "The kitten is curled up on my porch. I need to go shopping and pick it up some kibble soon." Nancy walked to her cupboard for a can of tuna to tide the thing over till she made it to the store.

"What kitten?" Edna's voice over the phone was terse and suspicious.

"The one from the alleyway last night, remember? I put it in the garage when I got in but it must have gotten out. Anyway, you were saying about a zoo?"

"Oh yes. So I called an old friend from the zoo; he and I are meeting for lunch today. I haven't seen him in ages. He was quite good in the sack, you know."

Nancy smiled. Edna didn't seem to have an off-switch for personal details.

"So you are consulting him about his expert sleeping skills?"

"Oh, no, he works with the large cats at the zoo."

"So what are you going to ask him about? Tigers?"

"Of course, plus any other juicy tidbits he cares to wing my way. I mean, isn't it strange to see a tiger downtown? There has to be a reason."

Nancy couldn't agree more, but she had another purpose, one that she wasn't quite ready to tell Edna about. The two hadn't had a chance to catch up on last night's activities and Linda's deathbed request. She had been all ready to tell her friend, but after the weird vibes she got from the figurine, she decided it might be a conversation left for another time.

Edna interrupted her thought. "I'll find out everything and drop by this afternoon when done. Oh, and don't worry about lunch. I'll bring you some."

"Turkey club with swiss," they said in unison.

Edna laughed. "You are too predictable."

"That I am, but before you go, can you look something up for me on the internet?"

Nancy hung up and stared at the number she had written down on the pad beside the phone. Edna's quick online search gave her the number of Linda's shop, a place called Ye Olde Herb Shoppe.

She dialed and listened to the number ring five times before the machine answered. She left a hasty message giving her name and number before hanging up.

Nancy tossed the phone onto one of the cushioned chairs next to her French doors that opened out onto the back patio.

Exiting to her backyard, she looked for the kitten. A rustling in the overgrown grass full of weeds told her where the scamp was hiding. She sighed as she surveyed the carnage. So many weeds this year, and she was getting too old to bend down to pull them. She walked over to retrieve the feline. "Come here, little one. Need to get you cleaned up like I should have done last night."

A small hand rake and a glove lying haphazardly on the ground caught her eye. She righted the small garden gnome that had fallen over before picking up the discarded tools.

More scatterbrained by the day. Nancy shook her head as she walked back to put away the items she had left out.

"Now that you have decided to adopt me, what shall we call you?" Tucked in the crook of her arm, the kitten purred loud enough that Nancy could hear it over the din of the local birds chirping all around her.

Edna bounced into the house with a shopping bag on one arm and a takeout bag on the other.

"Darling, you won't believe the day I've had!" Edna held out the bag of food to Nancy, who took it and pawed through it as she walked back to the kitchen island.

"Took you long enough. I nearly broke down and made lunch," Nancy said, scrutinizing the contents of the takeout bag.

"Sorry about that. Eduardo and I took a little longer than expected."

"Eduardo?" Nancy raised her eyebrow as she pulled out the paper-wrapped sandwich.

Edna plopped down in a chair at the small breakfast nook table and pulled off her shoes. "These dreadful things have to go in the trash."

Nancy was too busy delving into her sandwich to engage with Edna on the matter of non-comfortable shoes, but she did want to know about the zoo. The best way to get Edna to talk was to keep quiet. This time she had a grilled turkey, bacon, and swiss on wheat to help.

Edna tossed her shoes onto the rug and leaned back like she was in an easy chair. "You won't believe the dirt I learned. All those vicious deaths we keep hearing about in the news lately? I think they are all related to the tiger we saw last night. The police went to the zoo about four weeks ago asking if any large cats had escaped. Of course they hadn't, but the police were asking questions related to exactly what kind of damage a cat of that nature would do to a person and wanted specifics on where they would be hunting, living, et cetera."

Nancy nodded along. She'd had the same thought the night before when the beast was sitting on top of her hood. She still couldn't get over the notion that a predatory feline was roaming around the isthmus. She tried to ignore the fact that she and Edna came very close to being the next casualties. Someone had to own that thing; it was unrealistic for a tiger to evade capture in a city for so long.

"Well, of course the police have kept in contact since then. Eduardo said that they've had other killings. Interestingly, they are all older women, at least that's what the police have been telling him. Don't you find that strange? They never mentioned that in the news, did they?"

"They didn't. Very strange indeed," Nancy agreed. The whole thing didn't make sense. Tiger on the loose, killing old ladies. She thought back to the night before with Linda in the alleyway. Had Linda actually said *witches* were dying?

Nancy pushed the thought out of her mind.

Illogical ramblings of a dying woman.

"So here is the best part." Edna's grin reeked of gossip and whispers. She had dirt and it was eating her up not to tell it. "This isn't the first time Madison has seen a big cat on the loose, did you know this?"

Nancy instantly knew what Edna was talking about, and scolded herself for not remembering it. About a decade before, there had been a fighting ring among some of the very wealthy people of Madison. They would smuggle in illegal cats through Canada and fight them to the death. One of the cats got out and, being starved and tortured, had killed a mother and her young child before being put down by the authorities. It was a horrible tragedy and Nancy couldn't believe she hadn't made the connection until now.

She put down the rest of the sandwich, suddenly not hungry.

Edna had continued to drone on, telling Nancy the same thing she was thinking. "Eduardo thinks the smuggling ring might be to blame. He thinks it still might be going on. I have no unearthly idea why anyone would want to keep one of those things as pets. Dreadful creatures. Speaking of which, how is the kitten?"

Nancy leaned to the side and indicated the back door with a nod of the head. "You're welcome to go see her. I might call her Loki because of how mischievous she is. She keeps knocking down my garden gnomes."

Edna glanced at the door for a moment before looking back. "I'm sure she'll be fine outside. Oh, so did you call that place? Linda's shop?"

"I left a message earlier."

"Oh good. I thought the name was interesting. *Ye Olde Herb Shoppe*. That poor woman. The police aren't the only ones asking questions about large cats lately." Edna pulled up one foot and rubbed her arch. "So, about this rumored fight club in the area."

"It's horrible."

"I know. That's why we have to find them."

Nancy was glad she didn't have her mouth full of food, or Edna would be wearing a partially chewed sandwich right now.

"You're kidding, I hope?" Doing anything that dangerous was out of the question. Nancy was perfectly happy sitting at home. It was just a matter of time before Edna dragged her into something they wouldn't be able to escape. She thought about the previous night's activities. Going down that alley was the dumbest thing she'd done in the last year, but that had been different; she'd *had* to go.

"Just a small investigation, a peek around the secret curtain, if you will."

Nancy's mood darkened. "Absolutely not. We need to leave that to the authorities." She got up and looked out through the window to her front yard, mostly out of habit and to try to end the conversation. This whole thing seemed wrong. She shouldn't meddle in police business, but she couldn't stop thinking about what Linda had told her.

This is my task.

Edna didn't seem to care that Nancy had just shut her down. "Oh come on, Nan, aren't you a little bit curious?"

"I am, but looking up a fight ring? Don't you think that's a little much? We already survived one encounter with that thing, do you really want to make it two?"

Edna pursed her lips. "I suppose you are right, but the next time I want to do something crazy, you promise to follow along?"

Nancy knew she would regret it, but if she didn't give in to Edna's crazy once in a while, it would just get worse and worse.

"Fine. I agree."

Edna giggled with delight. "I'm going to hold you to it!"

Nancy's stomach tightened; she knew Edna would. Nancy turned to eye her car in the driveway, the noonday sunlight bouncing off the roof, reminding her of the scratches in the hood.

Nancy sighed. "You know my insurance company isn't going to believe this."

"They'll have to! Make sure to give them the police report number so they can look it up."

"Still," she mused, dropping the curtain and turning around, "after the last incident, I have to wonder if they are going to keep believing me. I promised I would stay away from farm animals."

"Well, that was hardly your fault. Who would have thought there would be an enraged moose loose in the streets of New Orleans? Besides, a tiger isn't a farm animal."

Nancy got a gleam in her eye. "Neither was a moose, yet there we were."

She would deal with the insurance company later, but thoughts about last night had her wondering about the figurine again. She had placed it in the library to put it out of sight. She wondered if she should tell Edna about it. The line of thinking got her wondering how she was going to find this Peter person. She did enjoy mysteries, but usually from the comfort of a good book and with all the lights on in the house. And the door locked.

Something about this one, though, made her want to do something stupid, like tell Edna what Linda had asked her in the alleyway.

Edna had always been a believer of, well, everything. The woman had faith in multiple gods, aliens, faeries, ghosts, and goblins. You name it, she believed it. She even had a psychic she saw on a regular basis. Nancy knew she was simply wasting money on the whole thing, but it made Edna happy, and it wasn't like Edna didn't have the money for it.

She thought about Linda's admonishment to find Peter. Nancy frowned.

If she told Edna about the promise made in that alley, then Edna would want to pursue this Peter guy. How much stock should she place in the promises made to a person on their death bed? The rantings of a dying woman were not exactly lucid. What led to that woman being torn apart by a tiger was the biggest question of all. Why a tiger?

Edna studied Nancy's face for a moment. Her countenance changed. "Uh-oh."

Nancy looked at her quizzically. "Uh-oh what?"

Edna pointed. "You have that look."

"What look?"

"The look you get when the answers don't add up."

"I don't have a look! Okay, maybe I have a look, but what could lead to a tiger stalking downtown Madison?"

Edna got up to refresh her tea. She grabbed Nancy's cup off the small table beside her on her way to the kitchen. Nancy followed her in.

She looked back across the front of her house to the library. "I …" she trailed off, her mind wandering. She wasn't exactly lying to Edna, but she felt like she should tell her. They rarely kept anything from each other. Maybe it was time to tell Edna.

Nancy opened her mouth when the phone rang.

Saved by the bell.

She picked up the handset on the wall and put it to her ear while she habitually grabbed the pad of paper and pen she kept close by. "Hello?"

"Hello?" It was a female voice. She had a thick Russian accent. "How you know my number? How you call me?"

"Anca? Anca Petran?" Nancy ventured a guess given the accent and the previous message she had left.

She grunted, irritated. Nancy decided to get to the point.

"My name is Nancy. I called Lin …um, the herb shop and after several rings it clicked over and I was able to leave a voice mail."

The woman on the other end of the line cursed. "What you want?"

"Well, this is going to sound strange, but I was with Linda last night when … well, she wanted me to contact you." It wasn't exactly true. Linda had told her to contact Peter, but she had said something about Anca, and Edna was right. Something was up and she wanted to get to the bottom of it. It wasn't normal for tigers to go around killing old women in the streets of her town.

"You were with my partner … er, Linda when she died?"

Nancy paused, collecting her thoughts.

"Yes, I found her in the alley before she … well, she passed." Nancy swallowed. Suddenly her mouth was very dry. "She wanted me to tell—"

"Not on phone. You come tomorrow," Anca interrupted.

"Oh, uh … okay." Nancy paused, searching for words. "I guess we could stop by tomorrow afternoon. Is it okay if I bring my friend?"

The woman agreed and gave her address and a time and promptly hung up when Nancy was only halfway done writing down the address.

"Well, that was strange."

Edna looked up, clearly oblivious to the conversation. "Huh?"

"That was Anca Petran." She glanced back at the library, feeling a sudden connection to the small jade cat. She remembered what she was going to tell Edna before the phone rang.

She is not ready yet.

The voice in her head came strong and powerful. It reminded her of the voice that had told her to go down the alleyway, or the one that told her to pick up the wine. She shuddered. Hearing voices was not normal.

Yeah, it could wait. She would tell Edna after the meeting.

"I guess we have a date with a dead woman's partner tomorrow."

CHAPTER 4

"YOU THINK THEY WERE LESBIAN?" Edna was hunched over the steering wheel of her newest BMW Roadster, a car that Nancy lovingly called her "post-middle-age crisis purchase."

Nancy replied, "Well, the word *partner* seems like a red flag, doesn't it? Besides, who are you to judge, based on some of the stories you refuse to tell me about your college years?"

Edna's cheeks flushed ever so slightly before responding. "So where are we going again?"

Nancy opened her purse to pull out the slip of paper that she had placed there. The figurine was on top of it and she had to move it to get to the paper. As she did, a slight coppery and earthy smell hit her senses, reminding her of Linda's death. Her stomach grumbled and twisted from the smell.

That was weird.

"I heard that. Lunch disagreeing with you?" Edna asked.

Nancy put her hand to her stomach. "Just caught the smell of something strange and my tummy rumbled."

Why had she even brought it? Part of her wanted to be ready to find this Peter fellow and return the figurine, but another regretted bringing it. Still, better prepared than not. Besides, if Anca and Linda were partners, wouldn't Anca know who Peter was?

The light turned green and Edna turned onto the road. "Okay, what's the number?"

Nancy's mind flashed back to two nights ago, on her knees in the wet muck, sobbing, while she watched the lifeforce of another human being drain out before her eyes.

"Nancy?"

Nancy grabbed the slip of paper again. She clamped the purse closed and zipped it up.

She tried to smile, but she could feel the unconvincingness in her voice. "Sorry, ever open your purse looking for something and you totally forget what it was?"

Edna huffed. "Sweetie, you ain't human if that doesn't happen to you at least twice a week."

Nancy read the address, watching the buildings pass her by. She pointed. "There it is, the theater."

Edna pulled over, a low whistle on her lips as she turned off the car. "I think we might be on the wrong side of the tracks here."

Nancy looked at her friend. "We're two miles from your house. In fact, we're on the same side of the tracks that you live on."

"Well yes, but I'm downtown, this is, well this is the edge of the warehouse district out here. Renovations haven't come out this far yet. This is … urban." Edna accent slipped at that last word.

Nancy stifled a smile. Her friend kept a check on her accent pretty well, but every now and again Nancy was treated to the southern drawl of Edna Maddox.

Edna wasn't kidding. The place was dilapidated. The well-weathered, redbrick buildings in front of her looked like old warehouses from the early 1900's. Three of them stood side by side along the road. Shops on the bottom, a row of arched windows looking out on the street on the second story. They were similar in style to the gothic arches adorning her home. The nearest building was home to a Chinese theater. A lightbulb encrusted sign that looked like a reject from 1950s Vegas hung precariously from the wall, waving and creaking in the breeze. The sign said *New Chinese Theater*. A restaurant and a Laundromat filled up the downstairs of the building to the left. Uncle Iroh's doors were wide open with three patrons sitting just inside, chatting away in an Asian language.

Nancy sighed, looking around the street, feeling suddenly reluctant to meet this curt woman in person. "Well, we better get this over with."

Edna opened her door. Nancy grabbed the handle of the passenger door, but something inside her hesitated.

She looked down. The small statue seemed to stare back through the heavy bronze zipper. She pursed her lips and frowned.

She stared at her purse for so long that Edna walked around the car and gazed at her through the passenger window.

Leave it here.

The voice sounded like it came from the backseat. Regardless of the origin, it sent chills up her spine. She put her purse on the floor of the car, kicking it under the seat so it wouldn't be visible, and opened the door.

Nancy was inundated with the smell of Chinese food and fish. The air was salty, despite not being near a sea, and heavy, almost like this section of town was under glass.

"This place is … interesting," Edna remarked.

Nancy looked at the address slip then back and forth between the two buildings ahead of her. Edna scratched her head.

"There's 545 and 549, but where is 547?"

A young Asian man wearing a WSU hoodie, backpack, and high-tops was blaring music through his white earbuds as he trotted out of Uncle Iroh's and into the alley between the two buildings.

Edna sneezed. Nancy cringed at the overly done cologne that lingered in the air behind the boy.

"Shit. I'm so stupid."

Taken aback not by the swearing, but by the unusual self-deprecation, Nancy queried her friend.

Edna pointed between the two buildings. "The address is down here."

Nancy looked between the two buildings, noticing for the first time in the darkness the metal staircase leading up to both buildings with doors beside them.

"You're kidding."

Edna squeezed her arm. "Not afraid of an alleyway, now are you, Nan?"

Nancy stuffed the address in her pocket. "Of course not! I don't have to run faster than the tiger, I just have to run faster than you."

They headed down the alleyway, darkness creeping in until they stood at the bottom of the wrought iron stairs. They went up a dozen steps to a landing, where it split, climbing to each side of the alleyway.

Nancy grabbed the railing and put her foot on the first step when a loud clang rang out from above. Both women jumped as the steel door to the apartment above the theater slammed shut, shaking the entire metal structure.

Edna rubbed her nose. "Well, I guess we better get this over with."

The two women walked up the creaky iron steps, finally coming to the steel door above the restaurant, and knocked.

Nancy barely touched her knuckles against the faded-gray steel door when it flew open outward. She jumped back to avoid getting hit.

A cacophony of smells hit her. Nancy wrinkled her nose at the exotic spices, heavy aromas of lingering smoke and burned incense. Her eyes watered from the particulates in the air. Nancy wondered if Anca cooked with an open-pit fireplace in her tiny apartment.

The room behind the door was dark, despite it being just after noon. For a moment, Nancy couldn't see more than a few feet into the apartment, but her eyes quickly adjusted, and she could see a woman holding open the door.

Anca Petran was short, plump, and ancient. Wrinkles, liver spots, scars, and burns all competed for space on her pale face, forearms, and feet poking out of her long woolen dress.

A patchwork of varying cloth was stitched together to keep the foregone dress together. Nancy wondered if she had any other dresses, as this one didn't seem to have been laundered in a long time.

"Nancy Moon?"

Anca's accent was thick and layered, almost lyrical. Bolshevik was the first word that popped into Nancy's head, and she nearly said it herself, but she caught her tongue and replied.

"Yes. And you must be Anca?"

The old woman, who had to look up well over a foot to see Nancy's five-and-a-half-foot height, squinted her eyes, almost like she was looking through Nancy rather than right at her. "You have spark but no knowledge. Did your mother not teach you? Inside. We talk inside. Both of you. Come, come in."

Nancy smiled courteously before taking a step into the apartment. As she did, she felt … something … tug on her, like the mass of air was somehow thicker inside Anca's doorway. It reminded her of going through a door into a supermarket on a hot summer day. Being hit by the blast of air conditioning was disorienting and cool. It gave Nancy the creeps. The feeling quickly subsided once she was inside.

It was only a step through the doorway, but it was like a step back in time. The apartment looked like it should have belonged in a museum. Nancy looked down at the old shag carpeting, seemingly the only thing from the twentieth century that belonged. There was no TV, not even a visible phone. Stacks of old newspapers and books filled nearly every surface, two—sometimes three—feet tall. Tossed on the floor was the newspaper Nancy had seen in the grocery store. The headline reminded her of how close she and Edna had come to being victims. Had Anca thrown it there in disgust after getting the call from the police?

"Sit on couch. I get you tea." Her voice wavered slightly, and Anca turned toward the kitchen. Nancy wondered how she was keeping her composure so well. Being old might help. The closer one got to the end of your own life the more cynical you tended to be about other people's death. Stark reality of getting old.

"Oh, this place is simply delicious, isn't it? Reminds me of Ushageeta's place." Edna reached out to touch a dusty globe that listed the countries in the Middle East as *Arabia*. Edna pulled back before touching.

Nancy nodded. "Wow, that's old." The knickknacks these women had collected were simply stunning. Edna sat down on the ancient Bridgewater couch while a bookshelf to the side provided a distraction for Nancy.

"Most of these books have actual leather bindings on them." Nancy ran a finger over a couple of the spines but pulled back with a start when one of them seemed to vibrate under her touch. She shook her finger at the sudden strange feeling.

"No touch my books, please."

Nancy whirled around. The woman managed to move around almost silently. Despite only being out of the room for a couple of seconds, Anca handed out small cups of steaming tea to her guests and pulled over a stool to sit in the middle of the room.

"I'm sorry, I used to be a librarian, so old books fascinate me. I love your place; so many antiques."

Nancy sat down next to Edna and held onto the cup with her fingernails, given there was no handle and the heat from the tea inside was already starting to burn her fingers.

"Thank you for seeing—"

Anca held up a finger, her eyes narrowed and she looked at Edna for a moment before studying Nancy. "How did you know her?"

"Linda?" Nancy asked, glancing quickly to Edna, who shrugged. Her eyes were wide with wonder.

Anca nodded briefly then chugged her steaming tea.

Nancy swallowed, inwardly cringing at the scalding liquid that must be pouring down that woman's throat right now. "Well, I, uh, I didn't know her. I only met her a couple minutes before she died. You see, a tiger came out of the alleyway and jumped on my car."

Anca held up the finger again. Edna was deathly silent to Nancy's right. Nancy felt like they were on trial somehow.

"Did she tell you who killed her?"

"Well, no, but I assume it was the tiger. It left blood on my car." Nancy's mind raced, then she got worried about something. "Did the police tell you what happened?" She suddenly felt apprehensive. Maybe Anca hadn't heard the full story from the police. She shouldn't be the one telling this woman about what had happened.

Anca looked inside her cup, then back up at Nancy. Her face and mood had changed. Where a stern glare had just been, there was softness, sadness, regret. "I know what happened."

Nancy let out a breath she hadn't realized she was holding. She was just starting to wonder what sort of person would be grilling the people who came to tell her about her late partner's last words, when Anca did an about-face.

"I ... I am sorry about the questions." Anca looked back down at her empty teacup and twirled the china around in her fingers. "Cannot be too careful, you know."

Nancy searched for words, but Edna jumped in.

"It's quite alright. Nancy and I both lost our husbands a few years ago. We understand how hard it can be."

Anca smiled shyly at Edna before nodding and getting lost in thought again. "Linda was a good woman." She stood and grabbed a photo book on the edge of the coffee table, sliding it to rest between the two women. On the cover was a picture of a much younger Linda and Anca. Linda wore hair in a very '60's flip style while Anca's braid hung past her hips. "We were much younger back then. Free love was in full-swing but still it was ..." She trailed off, her fingernail catching on the worn edge of the picture. "Still it was frowned upon to be lovers, even then. We had good life, you know?"

Nancy could feel emotions from her life with Richard welling up. She pushed them back down; now wasn't the time.

"We are very sorry for your loss," Nancy managed to say, her voice wavering. She thought back to her conversation with Linda in the alleyway. It seemed so long ago, even though it had only been two nights.

"So why were you worried about us? We're just a couple of old ladies," Edna asked.

Nancy shot her friend a look.

Anca smiled weakly. "To the point. I like you."

Edna smirked back at Nancy.

Anca sighed before picking up the photo book and placing it in her lap. She looked up, bearing a concerned expression.

"Did she tell you anything? About who killed her? Why she died?"

Nancy could feel the color drain from her face. Linda hadn't. She'd been so focused on giving Nancy a task to complete before she died. Nancy shook her head.

Anca continued. "The police haven't been telling this, but all the killings from that tiger are old women, like you and me." She wagged her hand back and forth between Nancy and her. "I don't know ... I needed to know that you are not part of the problem. Linda, she was a wonderful woman, but since she and I moved here, she has been very different.

"She opened up the herb shop, spending hours and hours down there, but she no make money. I think she started selling marijuana, you know? To make money? I worried for her. Worried for her life. I think she fell in with some bad men." Nancy was shocked. Everything about Linda was changing in her mind.

She almost expected the voice that had been haunting her to speak up, to tell her that this Linda was wrong, but nothing came.

"I'm so sorry. Did you tell the police?"

Anca nodded. "I tell them everything, I give them everything, but they don't believe. Linda had notes, see." Anca leaned to the side and grabbed a small pile of papers, passing a half sheet to Nancy. In neat blocky letters was an address, a date, and time. Nancy passed it to Edna.

"One in the AM, you see that?"

Edna let out a low whistle.

Nancy's mind reeled. Linda's secret life was starting to unravel. Linda selling pot? Still a tiger attack seemed kind of severe and oddly specific for drug dealers to use. Didn't they normally just shoot people who crossed them?

"Why did the police not take this?"

Anca shrugged. "They say they search the shop, find nothing. No evidence." She tapped her head with a pudgy finger, then her chest. "But I know, I feel. She was into bad things."

Anca stood. "More tea?"

Nancy realized she hadn't even touched her tea. She knocked it back quickly. The hot liquid still burned on the way down but had at least cooled significantly since they had started the conversation.

Anca took the cups and headed back to the kitchen.

Edna let out a stifled giggle.

"Oh no."

Edna frowned. "What?"

"We are not following up on this."

"But it's weed, Nancy. Don't you see? No one gets shot over weed anymore. Something doesn't seem right about this."

Nancy was about to say something when Anca came back in, bouncing slightly, holding three cups of tea. She was just handing them over when the door to the apartment burst open and a young Asian man ran into the room, panic on his face.

CHAPTER 5

H E CARRIED A STACK OF books, papers, and a handful of long bird feathers with black-stained sharp points. Quills? His floppy shoulder-length mane cascaded behind him as he carefully dodged around the clutter on the floor.

His voice was shrill and panicked. "Anca, I've gotten all those spells you've asked for. I haven't found the deed yet but I think it—"

He clamped his mouth as soon as he realized Anca wasn't alone.

Everyone in the room glanced around nervously for a tedious few seconds until Anca broke the silence.

"You can put them over there." Her voice and mood had changed drastically since talking about Linda. She seemed nervous. Her voice was quiet and subdued but had an edge to it, like she was trying to save face while telling someone they were wrong.

Edna cleared her throat. "Hi, I'm Edna."

Anca smiled nervously before motioning. "I'm sorry, everyone. Please sit. Nancy, Edna, this here is my … assistant. He, uh … he lives across the way above the theater."

The kid finished setting down the pile of papers on the floor near a door in the back wall and turned to face everyone. His face looked like he had just walked into the girls' room as a young boy and was terrified he was in the wrong spot.

He bowed slightly. "I'm sorry, Anca. I didn't know you had company." His features said he was Chinese or Mongolian, and he still had a hint of an accent, though it was hard for Nancy to pinpoint exactly what type of an accent it was; more West Coast than anything.

He bowed again, and turned to leave.

Nancy had a sudden thought pop into her head, a single word spoken by Linda that had been lingering there since the boy came in.

"Are you Peter?"

The young man, halfway back to the door, stopped mid-stride. He turned, his face stark as he met Nancy's eyes.

"Yes, my name is Peter." His voice had an edge of nervousness, like no one should know his name. He glanced at Anca, who shot him back an imperious look. He cringed.

Nancy smiled at the boy. "How old are you, Peter?" Could this be the Peter that Linda had talked about? Linda hadn't given any ages.

"I'm, uh, nineteen."

"And do you go to WSU?"

He nodded again, but not before glancing at Anca first.

Anca finally spoke up. "Peter, come join us. Nancy and Edna were talking about Linda."

He visibly perked up at the woman's name. "You knew Linda?"

Nancy suddenly didn't know what to do with her hands. "I was with her the other night … I found her in the alleyway and Edna here called 911."

His face grew red and scrunched up. He quickly wiped tears from his eyes before they could fully form as he sat down on the floor next to Anca. "It's so horrible what happened. I can't stop thinking about it."

Nancy knew the feeling all too well.

"Yes, we are all very hurt." Anca began to pet the boy's hair in a way that Nancy found a little unsettling.

The pit in her stomach was almost too much to bear. Nancy had to say something. "Peter." She glanced first to Edna then to Anca, and finally back to the boy. "When I was in the alley with Linda, she, well, she spoke to me."

"She did?" All three said in unison.

Nancy nodded and continued. "When I found her, she was still alive, but just barely. She mentioned you, Peter. She wanted me to find you. That's why I tried calling her herb shop and eventually spoke to you, Anca. I was actually trying to find someone named Peter and I didn't know where to go. I thought you might know."

Anca gave Nancy a look that made her second guess what she was about to say. She also became aware that she didn't have the figurine with her right now. She almost thought about asking everyone to wait so she could go down and get it from the car, but just thinking about it reminded her of the voice telling her it was not time, that she should leave it.

Edna spoke up. "You didn't tell me she spoke to you."

Nancy cringed. "I'm sorry, you and I didn't have much time to discuss things, and, well, I was still trying to process the whole thing."

"Did you tell the police?" Anca asked.

"I only told them that she said your name, Anca, which she did, and something for someone named Peter." She looked the boy up and down. He was holding hands with Anca, which seemed odd. Perhaps he was related to Linda? But why would Anca …? She pushed the thought out of her head. She was here to deliver a message.

"She said she forgives you, Peter. That's what she told me to tell you." *And give you a cat statue, but that's in my car.*

Peter looked to Anca, who stared back at him. They both had a stricken look on their face. Peter began to cry. Tears streamed down his cheek and he quickly wiped them and stood. "I have to go."

Another glance at Anca and he ran out of the apartment, leaving everyone in a stunned silence.

Nancy finally broke it. "I'm sorry, I didn't mean to upset him. Were he and Linda close?"

Anca gave her a curious look, like she was scrutinizing her for the first time, trying to find out if she was a threat or not. Her face softened. "They were. Her death has hit him very hard. His mother died when he was very young. He latched on to Linda as a mother figure."

"And now you?" Edna piped in. She had a manner to her voice that made Anca's words seem sexual.

Nancy nearly burst out laughing. Anca and him did seem to be a little touchy-feely. Him being nineteen and Anca being, how old was she? Certainly older than Nancy. Maybe eighty or ninety? It was kind of hard to tell with Anca. Nancy wouldn't have been surprised to hear this woman was over one hundred. She certainly had the wrinkled skin for it.

Anca pursed her lips. "He's very sensitive. Linda cared for him. I care for him."

The mood in the room was uncomfortable. Besides, who was Edna to say anything about hanging out with younger men?

Nancy stood. "Thank you, Anca. I think it's time we left. This was what I came to say. Will Peter be okay?"

Anca stood as well, followed by Edna. Both women's knees cracked. Anca had a melancholy look to her. "He will be fine. He's just going through a lot right now. Thank you for giving the message. He just needs time to process it is all."

Nancy understood the need to process information slowly. Four years later and she still struggled facing the fact that her husband wasn't coming back. Entire rooms in her large home hadn't been touched since he left. Nancy still had hope he would one day come back and pick up right where they left off.

"Did she say anything else? Give you anything?"

The statement caught Nancy completely off guard. She shook her head but the look on her face might have given her away. Linda had said other things and had given her something. Why would Anca know that, though?

Edna thanked Anca for her time, taking the lead to extricate them from what was becoming an uncomfortable conversation. Anca waddled ahead of them, leading the way out of the apartment.

As they passed the steel door set in the back wall, Nancy couldn't help but stop and look at it. Intricate geometric scrollwork adorned its surface, carved into the metal. The design was hypnotic. She reached out to touch it and pulled back as she felt a large spark in her fingertip.

"Please, no touch my door."

With that, she hurried along to catch up with Edna who was just leaving the small apartment.

Going out was worse than going in. Something about being in that apartment inhibited her emotions, like heavy blanket, suddenly removed. Her dulled senses suddenly came alive, as she was flooded with a whirlwind of emotion and senses.

She looked up. *Feeling* something in front of her. It was Edna's car … no, it was something inside Edna's car. *The statue.*

A longing for Richard filled her chest, melding with her conflicted projected emotions from the kid, Peter.

She started tearing up as she walked down the metal stairs. It was everything she could do to put one foot in front of the other. She couldn't explain what was wrong with her.

Was it that the reality of a woman dying in her arms had finally caught up to her? No, that didn't feel right.

Reaching the bottom, Edna turned, and her big, dopey grin melted when she saw Nancy's face.

"Oh my God, Nancy, what's wrong?"

Nancy found she couldn't speak. What the hell had just happened? One second she was walking out of the apartment and the next this wave of emotions had hit her.

She remembered the feeling of walking into Anca's apartment, that sensation of walking into a supermarket past a curtain of air. While she was in that place, her senses had been dampened somehow, but now that she was back out, she could *feel* things again.

She wiped the moisture from her eyes and looked at her friend. "I'm okay, just sad about everything going on."

Edna frowned and drew her lips into a line before grabbing Nancy's arm. "You are probably just overwhelmed. The incense in there was a bit much, even for me. Come on."

Nancy followed Edna back down the alley as she thought through the various conversations she'd had in the last two days. Linda's dying wish was for her to meet someone named Peter, tell him she forgave him, and give him a blood-covered jade cat statue. Nancy had done half of that.

As they neared the car, she thought about the statue. Anca had said that Peter lived across from her. Nancy turned back around and looked again at the staircase leading up between the two buildings. Anca's apartment was to the left, above the restaurant. Peter's would be to the right, above the theater. She could go give the figurine to him right now, and she would be done.

As Nancy opened the door and reached for her purse, however, the voice came back.

He is not ready yet. Be patient.

It gave her the creeps. The voice, something that had haunted her dreams for the last four years, had never spoken to her while she was awake until two days ago. Nancy didn't like it. Only, this wasn't exactly the same voice. It was different, more mature. It almost sounded like—no, that was ridiculous.

She glanced at Edna, who was getting into the driver's seat. Edna knew about the voice, and thought it was a ghost trying to communicate with her. According to her, ghosts didn't leave the world until their unfinished business was taken care of.

Nancy thought it was ridiculous, but she still shared it with Edna. The two shared everything.

Nancy squeezed her purse. *Well, nearly everything.*

Alright fine, she thought, half to herself, half to the voice. *Then when?*

No reply came.

Edna shut her car door, jolting Nancy out of her reverie. She looked up to the window that would have been Anca's apartment. The mustard curtains had been closed when they were in there just a few moments before, but they were parted now, and Nancy thought she saw something, a head with piercing eyes staring down at her.

"Nan?" Edna called out.

Nancy looked away for a split second to glance at Edna then back to the window. The face was gone. The curtain swayed side to side.

Nancy got into the car and held her purse tight as she glanced back up at the apartment over the restaurant. As she looked at the window, something inside of her seemed to light. A small flame, a burning question that needed to be answered. She had the urge to get out of the car and rush back up the stairs to talk to Peter. Maybe if she got to know him better, she would feel better about giving over the statue. She wanted answers to questions she couldn't quite formulate.

Edna broke the silence. "I have a confession."

The statement nearly startled Nancy, who was intently looking at the window. She turned, unable to keep from blurting out, "What is the confession?"

Edna gave her a strange look and Nancy returned a sheepish grin. "Sorry, I was just lost in thought and you startled me."

"Well, that slip of paper that she showed us, the one with the address and time on it? I took it."

"You didn't!"

Gears began whirring in Nancy's head. She'd wanted answers, hadn't she? Drug dealers, middle of the night meetings? It was all very intriguing and scary. The sane part of her wanted to turn that over to the police, but another part of her, that cold hard flame yearning to flourish, wanted to find out more about what was going on.

Edna had been telling her to get out more, hadn't she?

Something else about this whole situation bothered her. If Linda really was that mixed up with drug dealers, wouldn't the police have taken every shred of evidence to try to track down the killers?

She thought back to the night Linda placed that small figurine in her hand and told her to find Peter and forgive him. She could have said something about who killed her, but instead, that woman with her dying breath was trying to tell someone that they were forgiven. No, Linda didn't seem the type to be mixed up with drug dealers.

Given the six-hundred-pound tiger that had come barreling out of the alleyway with blood on its muzzle, Nancy suspected there was far more to this story than what was being reported in the newspapers. Something was going on and she wanted to know what it was.

"What are you smiling about?" Edna asked, her hands folded in front of her.

"I'm so proud of you, Edna."

"Proud?"

"Oh yeah, for stealing that paper."

Edna cocked her head slightly and squinted. "You're not saying that just to placate me, right? I have a feeling you are saying one thing but really meaning another."

"No, I promise, pinky swear, and cross my eye to die or whatever that is. I want to follow up on that slip of paper. Besides, I knew you were going to ask anyway, and I did promise I would agree next time you wanted to drag me on another crazy Ednaventure. So here is me agreeing."

"Really? Ooh that's scary." Edna studied the paper again.

"So when is the meeting?"

"Tomorrow night."

"You feeling like living life on the edge, Edna?"

Edna nodded furiously, her smile made her look like a kid in a candy store.

Nancy smiled reassuringly. "Let's do it."

CHAPTER 6

"N ANCY MOON." THE THIN MAN in the yellow trench coat and Coke-bottle glasses looked over a clipboard as he elongated her last name. He sounded like a talking cow with a cold.

"Hello, Josh." Nancy tried to keep the bile out of her voice. She grabbed a bundle of papers off the mail cubby by her front door and held them out at arm's reach. It wasn't that she was disgusted by him; it was that he didn't like getting too close to people. She supposed he was a pleasant enough fellow, if the ring on his finger was any indication, but Nancy still wondered if a real woman actually found him attractive or if he made so much money that *that* was what was attractive.

"So nice to see you again, Mrs. Moon. Fancy us talking again so soon."

Nancy's insurance claim adjuster had taken a vested interest with Nancy's account nearly two years ago, oddly soon after she had first met Edna.

"So you claim that a *tiger* jumped on your car three nights ago."

She watched the traffic meander by while she waited for him to look up from his clipboard and grab the papers.

She noticed an old blue Ford pickup sitting in the driveway of the house across Humboldt Lane.

Looking closer, she saw that the For Sale sign in the front yard was missing. Hadn't it just barely sold two days before? People didn't usually move in that fast, did they?

Sick of waiting for Josh to see what was right in front of his face, Nancy cleared her throat and waved the papers. "Ahem."

"Oh, well, I see." He grabbed the papers gingerly, like they were used tissues.

"It's all in the copy of the police report. Tiger fur in my windshield wipers and everything."

"You don't say. Well, we shall have to go take a look, shall we?"

You walked right past it to get to my front door; you couldn't have looked then?

"Sounds good, let's go."

Nancy tried to wait patiently while Josh meticulously scanned her car, judiciously snapping pictures with his digital camera. Nancy made sure to point out the two massive dips in the hood.

She looked at the blue truck again when she noticed someone familiar.

A young man in a WSU hoodie, head bobbing to unheard music, walked up the street to the bus stop. She never understood why college kids trekked so far from their university just to catch the bus stop close to her house. Maybe there was a marijuana supplier close by on her street. "Do you know how much longer this is going to take, Josh?"

"Oh I'm nearly halfway done here, Nancy Moon; you can't rush a thorough job, can you?

Of course you *can't.*

The bus at the corner of Humboldt and Vasher stopped at its station and a handful of college kids grouped together at the door.

"I understand thorough, Josh, but can't a couple of pictures be enough? You were just out here a couple months ago."

Josh straightened up and peered at Nancy over the rim of his thick, distorting glasses. "And that is precisely why I'm being so carful. You see, we aren't in the habit of losing money, but in your case"—he snickered—"well, you have quite the case. Besides, I love seeing your home. It's so unique."

Josh pushed the glasses to the top of his nose and continued to ramble on, but Nancy wasn't listening. She was too busy watching the commotion down at the street corner.

The bus driver was arguing with the kid in the hoodie. The kid pulled up his hands indicating he didn't have enough money for the fare. The bus driver pointed out the door and the figure, head hanging low, stepped off the bus and walked back down the street toward Nancy's house.

He had a familiar look to him, like she'd seen …

She recognized the swinging white headphones and the backpack.

"Um, Josh, do you need me? Can you finish up here on your own?"

Josh may have had a response, but Nancy was already walking down her driveway, watching the young man as his earbud cords bobbed to the beat of his walk.

Like most teenagers, he had a slump to him and was so oblivious to the world around him that he nearly stumbled into a dog being walked the other way.

She stopped at the end of her driveway before stepping onto the road in front of her house. Did she really want to get involved? Curiosity killed the cat and Nancy was out of her element here. She should leave well enough alone, but the words of a dead woman continued to haunt her.

Find Peter.

Linda's words lingered in her mind, even using the same voice. Nancy crossed the street, getting closer.

"Hey," Nancy yelled, nearly jogging to meet him before he got too far away. "I couldn't help but see you not able to get on the bus. Do you need a ride somewhere?"

He looked up at her, his countenance different from the distraught kid she had seen yesterday at Anca's apartment. He had been crying and emotional then, but today Peter looked happy and unfettered, despite the recent argument he'd just had with the bus driver. Peter looked at her, yanking out his earbuds. He looked around for a second, as if making sure that Nancy was indeed talking to him as if this was some sort of prank. "Uh, I don't have any money." He thumbed back over his shoulder toward the bus stop.

Nancy remembered their meeting just the day before. It had been a pretty rough day for him. She had almost gone back in to talk to him. Now she would get her chance.

"That's okay. If you can wait a few more bits for Mr. Speedy back there to finish with my car, I can give you a ride."

He looked at Nancy's car, then her house, then back to her. His shoulder-length black hair sticking out of his hoodie bounced from the motion. "Uh, sure, I guess."

Josh was just wrapping up with Nancy's car when she and Peter got back to the driveway.

The dents in her hood stood out as a stark reminder about the crazy last couple of days. She wondered if Peter would ask about them.

"Wait here a moment and I'll just head inside to get my purse."

He adjusted his bangs as Nancy looked into his eyes, which were dark like most Asian eyes but had a sparkle, a glint of something she couldn't quite put her finger on. They almost seemed to have small flecks of something else in them.

"Whoa," he said.

"Whoa?"

"Yeah, your house is really cool."

Nancy smiled.

"Yeah, like, I've walked past here a lot and I don't think I've ever noticed your house before. It's very different. Very unique."

Nancy's house was unique, that was for sure. Her husband's family had immigrated to this area over a hundred and fifty years ago and at the time owned most of the Madison area. But over the years of money management issues, divorce, remarriage, and deaths, they were forced to sell off more and more of the land until the family house, an aged gothic home was left with only a few acres surrounding it.

The ten acres across the drive to the north, the last vestige of the wooded area that had once been this town's milieu, was sold off by her husband in order to pay the debts that his uncle had left him when he inherited the house. Most of the homes in the immediate area were all built in the late sixties or early seventies. Nancy was there to watch the entire neighborhood spring up around her as a woman in her early twenties.

To say her house stood out was an understatement, but what was even more unique was that even though it didn't match the rest of the homes in her neighborhood, most people didn't seem to notice. Once they did, they had a bunch of questions. She thought it odd that in a sea of mid-century tract houses, her mammoth three-story gothic home with its spires, gable roof-line, arched windows, and cupolas didn't stand out. She initially thought the neighbors had just gotten used to the look of her home on the skyline, but soon she realized that there was something odd about her property.

People didn't notice her house until they were on her property. It was the oddest thing, but one she soon learned to deal with as construction guys, delivery folk, and others would stop and gape at her house as soon as they got into her driveway, much like Peter was doing right now.

She had shrugged it off as some quirk of the people in the area, but Edna had different opinions. She said the house was spelled, something Nancy and she had had more than one heated conversation about.

Still, she had to admit the last few days had been hard to explain with observable data. Tiger in Madison, Linda saying that witches are dying, and now voices that had only ever haunted her dreams now seemed to haunt her everywhere she went.

Peter continued to gawk while she ducked into her house and grabbed her purse, which she had left in the library. She opened it up and took a look inside. The heavy green statue of the cat stared back at her.

She looked back out at the young man still gaping at her slate roof. Nancy still hesitated. Something about walking out to hand it to him right now seemed wrong. She felt like there were still unanswered questions.

What if it was the wrong Peter? Peter was a fairly common name, and while this boy certainly topped the list of suspects, it was possible there was another Peter in the mix. Maybe Linda had meant a drug dealer? Nancy shuddered at the thought.

But more than just the name being similar, Linda had said he was trapped, and something about him being ready. She also said it would help him, somehow.

That was enough for her. While she was fairly sure it was the correct Peter, her meeting with him yesterday did raise an eyebrow or two. What was a nineteen-year-old kid doing hanging out with someone in her eighties? Unless she was his grandmother, it just seemed odd. Nancy needed to learn more about this boy, and driving him home would give her that opportunity.

She grabbed the figurine out of the purse and tucked it into a drawer in her roll-top desk. She wouldn't jump the gun until she sorted out some answers first.

She glanced out the window. Peter was waving goodbye to Josh as he drove away.

At least he seems like a nice young man.

"So, you go to WSU?" They had just pulled out of the driveway when Nancy figured he was trapped enough to start with the questions.

"Uh, yeah."

"And what do you study?"

He thought for a moment. "Acting."

"Oh, well, that's very cool. So tell me where you are from, Peter."

"From?"

"Yeah, did you grow up here in Wisconsin or did you move?"

Kids ... it's like pulling teeth to get information.

"Oh, I'm from California, San Francisco area. I came here to study."

Nancy was finally able to place the accent she had been hearing. "Are the studies going okay?"

Peter nodded. "They are. At least they are for me."

"For you? Why do you say that?"

"Well, my father doesn't completely agree with me being out here. Or with the degree."

"Your parents don't like the degree?"

"No, well it's my father only. My mother … she died years ago."

"Oh my, I'm sorry to hear that." Nancy remembered Anca telling her that the day before.

"Thanks. I was pretty young when it happened, so I don't really remember her."

"And your father never remarried?"

"No, he's a bit of a loner. I think he and mother got along okay, but I sometimes wonder if he even misses her." Nancy saw melancholy set in over Peter's expression.

"I wouldn't read into that too much. Married couples can be odd, especially when children are involved; we have our own ways of expressing or bottling up our emotions." Memories of Richard tugged at Nancy's heart. She shoved them aside to focus on Peter.

"Yeah, I can see that."

Nancy hesitated, not sure she should ask it, but she finally did. "So what studies would your father prefer you do?"

"Actually he didn't want me going to college."

"Oh." She kept driving, not sure what to say to that. From the corner of her eye she could see Peter smile. Nancy suddenly felt flushed.

"I bet you weren't expecting that, huh? Asian father, figured he wanted me to do math or physics or something? No, he's actually a sculptor. He is really good at statues and figurines. My mom used to help sell them before she died. He wanted me to go into the family business like my two older brothers. He said I don't need college to be successful."

Nancy thought about that for a second. Part of her wanted to interject saying how important an education was, but she also knew that you didn't have to be well educated to be successful. Some of the most well-known billionaires were college-dropouts. Besides, he knew how important it was. Why else would he be here on this side of the country, going to college?

Her heart fell at the sight of the look in the boy's eyes. He was in pain. This was not just grief over losing someone he cared about either, someone had told him to not discuss Linda or her death, and that was not right.

"I'm sorry if I brought up things I shouldn't have. I didn't mean to hit you with something out of the blue, it's just that, well, I was the only one in the alleyway that evening and I was just hoping to get some more information about her is all. Someday when you're ready to talk about her, though." Nancy smiled weakly, trying not to seem too eager. "I can't help but shake my head at her being caught up with drug dealers, though. Such a shame."

That got his attention. "What? No. She never sold drugs. She had people in her store every other day asking for pot on account of it being an herb shop, but she hated the stuff, she would have never sold it." The passion was back in his eyes. Two stalwart flames burning with assurance.

Nancy half expected this answer and was glad she had pushed him a little bit. "Oh, good. Well, I'm so glad to hear that rumor is false. You know how old women like to gossip. It was getting around, but I'll be sure to squash that rumor like a bug next time I hear it." She paused, collecting her thoughts. "Thank you Peter."

He smiled tentatively and nodded briefly. "It's not that I don't—" A loud metallic bang echoed in the distance and Peter cut his sentence off, looking down the alleyway with a wild look in his eye.

"Something wrong?"

He was silent for a bit then finally, in a voice that seemed too nervous for such a young man, replied. "It's fine, it's Anca. She'll be looking for me to help with her studies."

She bent down, following his gaze. Anca Petran was shuffling down the stairs in the alleyway.

Nancy put her hand on Peter's forearm again. He reflexively tensed but relaxed after a moment. She considered inquiring further, but Anca was staring at them with a grumpy look from the darkness of the alleyway. Nancy decided to let the poor boy go and implement another plan.

"Well, you're here, safe and sound. Delivered as promised."
She grinned widely and waved at Anca.

"Yeah, thanks for the ride; sorry I didn't have any money."

"Not a problem at all. If you ever need another ride, you
know where to find me. Oh, and one more thing, if you don't
mind. Do you have a job?"

Peter looked confused.

"I mean how do you earn money?"

"Oh, well I do odd jobs here and there; mostly I'm here on
scholarships, though. I help out the theater group in my building
with lighting and other things, set building and the like, they cut
me a break on my rent and I help out for some money here and
there. Why do you ask?"

Nancy tapped with her fingers on her pursed lips. "Because I
think I have a job for you if you are interested."

CHAPTER 7

"O VER THERE. RIGHT IN BETWEEN those two trucks."
Nancy pointed to the side of the dingy road. "I still can't
believe we are doing this." Nancy knew the reason,
though. If she hadn't suggested it, Edna would have wanted to
come anyway, and Nancy wouldn't allow Edna to do this alone.
Plus, she had to admit she was a bit curious.

"Oh, it'll be fine. We're just here to observe from a distance."

As hesitant as Nancy might have been, and despite all the
butterflies in her stomach, she was glad she came. Besides, she
wouldn't forgive herself if something had happened to Edna and
she wasn't here to help.

"So what are we looking for?" Nancy filled in the silence
that was beginning to permeate the car's cabin.

Edna pulled out the slip of paper she'd stolen from Anca's place.

Why would Anca have held onto a piece of paper that detailed
a late-night meeting for a drug deal from her dead partner? Why
hadn't she given it to the police as evidence for the murder
investigation? Past that, why show it to two complete strangers?
Nancy was sure something was up, but didn't want to say anything
about Anca yet. She wanted to confirm her suspicions first. The
conversation with Peter earlier that afternoon had cleared up a few
things in her head, and she was hungry for more answers.

Something bigger than an old woman's bizarre death was
going on. Maybe this paper would help her piece together some
of the puzzle. Nancy yearned to know the answers. Answers

were the main reason she even considered the notion of coming out to something potentially dangerous.

I will find answers to your riddles, Linda.

She had made a promise to a dying woman and she intended to fulfill it. But that didn't mean she wasn't scared.

Edna interrupted Nancy's thoughts. "There, I think." She pointed to a rundown old gas station half a block away on the other side of the street.

Edna turned to Nancy and grabbed her arm. "Oh, this is so exciting, isn't it?" As she turned on her phone, the light shone into Nancy's eyes.

"You should probably turn off the phone so they don't see the light."

"Oh yeah, that would be bad, huh?" Edna hit the power button on her smartphone with an audible click and stuffed it away. "Good thing I was done with it. We really should get you one."

"You already did, don't you remember? For my last birthday."

"I did? Well, why aren't you using it?"

Nancy gave her friend "the look," hoping it was enough. Nancy and technology did not mix. Like oil and water. Only her oil was on fire and filled with flame-retardant hornets. It was one of the reasons she still drove her Edsel. The thing worked like a charm all these years. She didn't need any fancy buttons and LED lights. She just needed a car.

"I almost forgot." Edna held out a thick bracelet to Nancy.

"What's this?" Nancy took it with a bit of trepidation.

"It's a secret bracelet. I picked these up a while back and have been dying to use them." Edna produced another one, roughly the same size and thickness as the one she had handed Nancy, but with more psychedelic colors. She unclasped the bracelet but instead of putting it on her wrist, she pushed on two sides and a small blade popped out where the buckle was.

"Ooh, now that's fancy."

Edna winked. "I know right? I figured we're doing undercover detective work; we needed some protection." Using the carpet of her car, she retracted the blade and donned the concealed-weapon bracelet.

"So you never finished your story with Peter."

"Oh that, well nothing much else. After dropping him off, I asked him if he wanted a job cleaning out my attic and he said yes."

"Your attic, huh?" Edna's tone was caring and serious. Lost were the hits of whimsy. "It's good to see you finally moving on, Nan."

Nancy pursed her lips. She didn't want to have this conversation again, not here. Edna did seem to care, she just didn't understand. Nancy sighed. "Thanks, and you're right. I know." She put her hands up in the air like she was being held hostage. "I admit it. I've been dragging my feet on this for a far too long."

"It's what I've been saying for two years now and what Maria said before that."

Maria. Nancy hadn't heard that name in a while, and Edna rarely brought her up unless she was trying to really make a point. The counselor at their grief retreat had been a nice enough woman, and Nancy had come out of the retreat with a renewed vigor for life and the resolve to change.

"Well, Maria was right. Make sure to hunt her down and tell her. Besides, I found what I needed at that retreat anyway." She smiled and Edna winked.

"Aren't you sweet? I agree. So what do we do here?"

"We wait." Nancy hoped the grief counseling line of questioning was over.

"No entertainment while we wait? I wonder if there is a mobile dancing guys cabaret. Is it a cabaret if it's all guys?"

Nancy stared blankly at Edna. She sighed. "You know, I'm not sure. I should look that up when we get back, assuming we're still alive."

Ignoring the jab, Edna continued. "I've heard of an all-male review. Maybe it's a cabaret if it's female dancers and a review if it's male dancers? Lemme check." Edna pulled her phone out of her purse.

A sharp pang of fear knifed Nancy in her stomach. Waves of panic burrowed up her spine, like a sea of termites gorging on wooden flesh. It was like a new sixth sense had awoken inside of her and she was still getting used to this new vestigial appendage. She wanted to do some self introspection. Re-evaluate her existence, but now wasn't the time.

Something was out there, watching her.

Nancy grabbed Edna's wrist, halting her movement. "Put that away." Her tone was deathly quiet but stern.

"What's wrong?" Edna whispered back.

Nancy knew what it was and where to look. Terror gripped her at both the reality of what she was looking at, and the fact that she somehow knew where and what it was before checking.

She wasn't sure which terrified her more.

"The tiger is watching us."

Edna gasped. "Where?"

Unless she had known where to look, Nancy wasn't sure she would have ever noticed it, but the unmistakable outline of a large jungle cat was visible just behind the tall grass on the side of the mini storage units across the street.

"Left side of the warehouse, see those tall bushes?"

Edna nodded, remaining silent.

"You can barely see its eyes in the middle of the bushes, but look at the ground. See the shadow?"

"Sweet Mary, Mother of Joseph," Edna breathed once she noticed the shadow. She gripped Nancy's hand to the point that it hurt.

"How did you see that thing?"

Nancy wasn't willing to take her eyes off it. "I don't know. I just got this feeling of being watched; I looked up and there it was."

"That's pretty creepy, Nan."

"I know, but that's not the least of our problems."

"What now?"

"Our drug dealers have arrived."

A mideighties Chevy pickup truck with a large wooden container in its bed rolled up a few buildings down from them.

Headlights were off, and unfortunately there wasn't much lighting from that distance to help Nancy see what was going on. She squinted but wasn't able to make out the actual color of the truck, it being in shadow. Movement inside the truck indicated there was more than one passenger. By the look of it, the entire cab was filled with people.

"What do we do?" Edna hissed.

"Nothing, lay low, and hope to God everyone ignores us. Maybe the tiger will kill them?" They were halfway down the next block, so far out of the way and in shadow that they should be able to stay hidden or start the car and make a getaway if anyone came running.

"You're assuming they don't control the damned thing."

Nancy had thought about that but chose to hope that the tiger would help them out of this situation. Worst case, the dealers had guns and they would be more apt to chase her and Edna down in their car. A tiger would be easier to deal with as long as she and Edna never got out of their car.

The truck door opened but movement to the side caught Nancy's attention. She looked back to where the tiger had been but saw nothing besides shaking foliage.

Edna let out a minuscule gasp.

"How many do you see?" Nancy asked, scanning the area for signs of the tiger. Something inside of her told her that it had left when the men showed up. She wasn't sure if that was a good or a bad thing.

"Two, I think, big guys by the look."

Nancy looked at Edna's face. "I thought last time we went to the eye doctor your eyes were worse than mine."

Edna turned slightly and winked before tapping the horn rim of her glasses with the tip of her "did" fingernails. The fake, spiraling gemstones embedded in the paint glinted briefly off the streetlights. "I asked them to up my prescription a tiny bit, so now I see at 20/15 instead of 20/20."

Nancy smiled. "Oh Edna, when will you learn? You're supposed to grow old gracefully."

"Oh hell no! You go into it kicking and screaming and fighting it every step of the way. You punch it in the face and tell it to go cry to its mama."

"Wow." Nancy's reply toed the line between genuine and sarcastic. She sat back in her seat, her fingertips resting on the end of her nose while she pursed her lips beneath the triangle of her fingers.

"Wow?" Edna looked between Nancy's eyes and her hand. "Did I miss something?"

"No," Nancy replied after a brief pause, keeping the same tone. "I just never knew how much of a philosopher you were. I should write that down. Embroider it on a pillow."

Edna smacked Nancy on the arm. "Oh, bite me."

"Sometimes I wish I could."

Edna's cackle made Nancy cringe. She watched as two big men climbed out of the pickup across the street; the vehicle visibly rising as their weight left it.

Nancy pointed. "You're right, two of them, and they are big guys."

Huge was more like it. Nancy wondered how both men had managed to fit beside each other in the full-size truck's cab.

Nancy frowned at her failing vision.

One of the big guys pointed somewhere to the side of their truck and the other guy headed off that direction.

Suddenly Edna's phone rang. Both women jumped.

"Turn it off!" Nancy whispered loudly.

Edna clamped down on the power button, silencing the ringer, then proceeded to lower the volume on her phone down to silent.

"Who the hell is calling you at one in the morning?"

"Eduardo."

"The zoo guy?" Nancy couldn't believe it. Edna's booty-call was going to get them killed.

Edna gave a cheesy grin. "Tiger research?"

Nancy raised an eyebrow. "I think he knows enough about large hairy cats, Edna."

The two burly men came back to the truck, gyrating their hands in such a way that make them look like they were talking to each other. One of them peered in the direction of Edna's car, but Nancy and Edna had found a good spot deep in the shadow of the old Oscar Mayer plant, and with the custom midnight-blue paint job of Edna's BMW, it would be nearly impossible to see them from that distance.

I hope.

"I wish I'd brought binoculars," Nancy said, squinting at the men in the distance.

"I agree." Edna paused. "Oh wait!"

She pulled her phone up to her eyes and turned on the camera app, then using two fingers, zoomed in on the image of the two men in the distance.

It was a bit fuzzy in the low light, but Nancy could see the men a lot better now.

Their pale skin shone in the moonlight as they approached. The burly fellows, true to meathead fashion had cropped blonde hair. Each was white with no discernible neck, only broad shoulders that turned into a beefy head with deep-seated eyes and distorted facial features, presumably from multiple broken bones. They looked like boxers back in the day before safety regulations required better padding for the sport.

"I wish I could hear what they were saying. You don't happen to have an app for that, do you?"

Edna shook her head. "No, but at least we have their faces. I might be able to—"

Edna moved a finger and pressed one of the buttons on her phone. That is when all hell broke loose.

A large flash went off in the car.

Edna shrieked and dropped her phone, which landed on the floor of the car with a clunk. The flash of the camera was still on, filling the cabin with light and blinding Nancy. Both Nancy and Edna reached for the phone, bumping heads in the process. Nancy managed to grab it first, covering the light with her hand. She shoved the phone into her purse and zipped it as fast as she could.

"What did you do?" Nancy whispered loudly.

"I'm sorry! I didn't think it would flash!"

Nancy could feel her temper rising, but it wouldn't do any good to scream at Edna, who clearly felt bad. Everyone makes mistakes. They just needed to recover from this one and hopefully not die in the process.

"I think they're coming over here," Edna stated, her voice even and dry.

"Drive!"

"I dropped the keys and I can't see them without the light!" Edna's voice became shrill and frenzied.

Panic circled Nancy's head like a pair of starving sharks. The two big men had already closed half of the gap between their truck and Edna's car.

What were they going to do?

"Give me the phone." Edna's tone was insistent.

"What? So you can turn back on the flash and get us killed?" Nancy gripped her bag closer.

"No, silly. They already know we're here. We might as well own it. I have a plan."

Nancy dreaded those words every time they came out of Edna's mouth. They were words of caution to her at this point, words that could change her fate in the briefest of moments. Nancy hesitated, her thoughts running wild, but she grabbed the phone and shoved it back into Edna's hand.

The two locked eyes for just a moment before Edna flashed her pearly whites. Nancy regretted her decision already.

"Follow my lead," Edna said with her patented Naughty Grin plastered on.

The two men were fifty feet from the car, and Edna was flashing the camera in odd intervals. She leaned in to Nancy and put her arm around her, taking the odd selfie every handful of seconds. The flashes were blindingly painful in the stark absence of light or any plan.

Nancy groaned inwardly. Edna was right. The men already knew they were there. It would be better to diffuse the situation than run away from it. She hoped.

The men split up, one going to the front of the car, while the other stopped outside the driver window before knocking with his beefy knuckle. Edna ignored the knock and kept flashing selfies.

The second knock came harder, more insistent. The man at the front of the car folded his arms across his meaty chest.

Nancy got a much better look at him now. He wasn't just big boned, he was heavy as well as muscled, like a professional wrestler or one of those guys who pull cars with their teeth for a living.

Sitting with Edna in the car at half past one in the morning with two twenty-something thugs standing on either side of their car, Nancy forced herself to not be terrified and lose it.

A third, more insistent rap came from Edna's window. The meaty guy in front put his knuckles on the hood of the car and pushed down. Nancy felt the car pitch forward, her stomach lurching in anticipation. It wasn't so much the speed or distance, but the threat was real. This man was powerful and was able to bend the shocks of a brand-new luxury sedan.

Edna casually lowered the window all the way.

"It's about time you showed up," Edna yelled before the guy next to her could say anything.

"What you say?" The man at her window, also about the same age, had a Northern European accent. It was thick and gravelly, like it had a lot of hair to go through to leave his mouth. It was the voice of someone who had lived a hard life. A stony life. The two men shared a lot of similar features.

"I said, it's about time you showed up. Payment up front," Edna looked between the two men, who now looked like brothers to Nancy. "And where are your dresses?"

"Dresses? Vidar, you hear anything about dresses?"

Vidar pulled his fists off the hood of the car, which relieved Nancy more than she thought it would. There was something about that threat of physical violence that unnerved her terribly.

Edna interjected. "Yeah, I thought if we were going to do this thing, we'd all be in dresses. You said you like to dress up."

The two men glanced at each other again, a silent conversation between them. The one at the window stooped down and peered in at the two ladies.

"I think you should get out of your car."

"I'm not getting out until you pay for our services."

"Services?"

Edna cackled. "You called us asking for two older ladies to dance with. You said you'd be cross dressers. Now I'm not one to judge. If us old broads are what get you two off and you want to meet at one in the morning to avoid the gaze of whoever you're afraid might see, then I'm all for it, but I gotta get paid first. It's just business."

The man looked confused then stood up straight to talk to his partner in crime, who was slowly walking around to Edna's side of the car. "Vidar, they're whores."

"Hey!" Edna snapped at him. "Don't you dare call me a whore! I'm a business professional and I'm damn good at my job. I'm not judging you for your lifestyle, so don't you dare do it to me, you hear? What's your name, son?"

He looked bewildered. "Martin," he said after an awkward pause.

"Look, Martin, we have other clients meeting us at three, so are we going to do this or not? We could knock out a couple quickies between now and then if you're not gonna pay."

Martin stood up and scratched his belly. Vidar got to the window and peered in. Nancy tried her best to look as casual and as bored as possible, while Edna groaned.

"Check out the package on this one, Candy. I wouldn't want that thing near me. Course, being so old, it'd be a hot dog down a hallway, am I right?" Edna elbowed Nancy rather hard and began cackling before devolving into a fit of coughing brought on by too many years of smoking.

Both brothers looked at each other and spoke in a Scandinavian tongue.

Nancy finally spoke up, wishing she were missing a few teeth at this point, which might have helped sell the old French whore schtick. She worked on scratching up her voice and raised it an octave and a half for dramatic effect. "Well, what'll it be? We don't have all night. We doing this or not?" She cringed inwardly at the hellish harpy voice that came pouring out of her mouth and hoped she'd keep her composure while they processed the question.

The two boys looked at each other, then Vidar spoke. His voice was lower than the other's. Gruffer.

"You two better get out of here. I think you might be on the wrong street."

Edna put her hands up in defeat. "Okay, okay. We'll mosey on out of here. No harm done."

The two men said something else to one another and turned to walk away. As soon as the windows sealed shut Edna burst into a peal of laughter.

Nancy went white with worry but couldn't help smiling herself. "We better get out of here while we still can. Don't want them coming back."

Edna settled down and, agreeing with her friend, started the car and drove off.

Being invisible was tiring, but Dragon rarely got to use his powers in front of others. He'd been cooped up for far too long. He had gone stealthy the second he sensed *it* as they drove up.

Office work was so mundane, and being out for the first time in weeks was satisfyingly liberating. He preferred to be outside. Office world kept him on too tight a leash.

Imagine his surprise at smelling the beast out here, so late at night. The thing was making a ruckus around town and if Dragon didn't get it under control, others would start noticing.

The thought unnerved him. He needed to get this locked down fast. It had gone on too long already. He only hoped his contribution to this mess would be easily swept under the rug.

"Hookers, eh?" Dragon had more important things to worry about than a couple hookers out too late and in the wrong area, but he couldn't pass up the chance to make Vidar nervous.

"They weren't who we were looking for." Vidar's voice wavered as he looked around for his boss.

Dragon silently circled the two brothers, thinking through ways he could pester the large brute more than he already was. A rustle to the side caught his attention and he turned to look.

"Yeah Vidar, but the one, she—" Martin's sentence was cut off abruptly by Vidar punching him in the shoulder.

"Shut up, Martin," Vidar hissed.

The faint rustle around the corner of the abandoned gas station immediately stopped at the thump of Vidar's fist on his brother.

Damned trolls.

Dragon crept over to the bushes, toward the spot he'd felt.

It was empty, of course. He'd been too careless so far. Let the two morons talk for too long. He'd lost his chance.

The smell of the beast still lingered. He scrunched up his nose at the stink.

"Fuckin' therans. Stink like a bastard." Dragon unzipped his pants and pissed on the slightly trampled spot of grass. "I'll find ya and I'll gut ya and I'll hang ya on my wall."

Padding along in the dead of the night, the tiger was king of the urban jungle. After the car drove away, it slunk up to where they had conversed with the bad men. One of the women wore such strong perfume that the tiger sneezed.

The tiger kept its mouth open as it breathed in the scent over and over, memorizing the fine portions, so as best to differentiate her from the other woman.

The women's scent filled the cool morning air, and it could follow it back to where they lived. Where *she* lived.

Twenty minutes later, it found the large house. Lights on the ground floor were out.

The tiger hunched by a blue truck, watching as the smelly woman tried to get into her car then turned around and went back to the house. She paused by the front door then disappeared around the side. A minute later she came back around, got in her car, and drove away.

The tiger crouched down, its stomach barely touching the cold pavement. It would need to move fast when it could. It waited for the final light to go out.

Its movements were swift and calculated. Smooth and refined. This was its natural element; this was what it lived for.

The hunt.

It prowled forward, the edge of its whiskers just brushing the blue pickup's bumper. A quick look side to side to make sure the coast was clear and it was off, bounding across the pavement, clearing the road in less than a second. The touch of cool grass felt good under its paws, so used to bloodying themselves on hard concrete and pavement.

It slammed into an invisible wall just before it got to the front door.

Pain shot through its body and it crumpled to a heap on the ground. It let out a mournful cry for a moment before righting itself. Soon it was pacing back and forth, testing the unseen barrier. It found no entry, no way around. Leaping into the backyard over the fence didn't help, and it found a fierce group of bewildering lights that chased it away. Nasty things, pointy and spiteful. They chased it from the yard, poking its hind leg repeatedly.

Dejected, the tiger limped away, alone, afraid of its master not understanding. It had to report back.

CHAPTER 8

MOST BIRDS WERE PLEASANT. THEIR cheery tones and chatter among peers brought Nancy joy as she watched them dance among the trees or skitter across the ground after seeds.

What she didn't appreciate were the loud, obnoxious ones that wouldn't stop making persistent and grating squawks, like they were choking on a frog.

This latter was the sound that bored into Nancy's slumber and jerked her awake into the most unpleasant mood.

She threw off the covers and stumbled out of bed. Looking in the mirror didn't do much to help. The demon that stared back at her needed to be cast back to the hell that she had flown in from. "That is the last time I go out past midnight with that woman."

Attempts to detangle her unruly peppery hair failed miserably. Sighing, she dropped the brush back on the counter and moved toward the door to her bedroom.

It was open, which was surprising for her, given she normally was very careful to keep her door closed, but she got in late last night … no … it was this morning that she got back, wasn't it?

She glanced at the clock hanging on the wall. She was making a habit of sleeping in.

Sighing, she walked out of her bedroom. The carpet runners down the hallway of her second-story balcony felt cool to her bare feet, another odd thing in a string of oddities for this morning.

The damned bird was even louder out here. She winced at the piercing notes. It was way too early and far too loud. She would investigate, but she needed coffee first.

Cursing Edna's name under her breath, Nancy descended the steps. She ran out of swear words halfway down and had to recycle them again. She chose to go backwards through the list.

Nancy.

The voice was decidedly female, distant, and pained. It lingered in her ears like an echo. It was hauntingly familiar, like a bad dream.

She listened over the deep thump of her heart in her chest and the whooshing sound of blood through her ears, trying to keep her breathing calm and even. She couldn't hear anything other than traffic noise.

The air down here was much too cool, like she had left a window open on accident. It had been a late night, so she wouldn't put it past herself.

Either I'm going crazy or I'm hearing voices. Maybe both.

She spun around, catching a glance of her wild expression in the foyer mirror. "Who's there?"

No response.

A sickly smell of tar and grass hit her nostrils. She turned up her nose and glanced at her front door. The silver handle glinted back at her in the morning light. The door was locked, which did nothing to calm Nancy's escalating fear.

She shook with apprehension. "I will call the police!" Her voice held confidence, interrupted by only a thin waver of doubt at the end as her true emotions bled in.

She heard a noise, a slight erratic clicking sound down the hallway. She looked around for a weapon. She grabbed the black umbrella out of the bin next to the front door, holding it in front of her like a sword.

Her memories flashed to the dream she'd been having just before she awoke, of the giant tiger attacking her in an alleyway in the middle of the night while a woman in blue screamed at the sight. A shiver ran up her spine.

Nerves on edge and her vision red with anticipation, she rounded the corner, umbrella thrust in front her. Something moved in the shadow, sending her nerves into overdrive.

"Yaaaa!"

The roar was reciprocated, but only from a far smaller creature than what haunted her dreams of late.

It was Loki, the tiny kitten; fur bristling, tail erect, and claws extended. The noise was not one of anger, or malice, but of sheer terror. Its tiny claws searched furiously for purchase in the nicks and gouges of the aged wood flooring. It raced away from her and ran around the corner, out of sight.

Nancy stood for a long moment, umbrella outstretched, trying to catch her breath, soothing her nerves and heartbeat.

She dropped the umbrella and smiled, hand to forehead at the ridiculous turn of events this morning.

"Come here, little one," she sang as she reached down, twiddling two fingers around the corner.

Meow.

The sound had some hesitation in it, but soon Nancy felt the soft, warm, and wet nose of the kitten against her finger.

"Which one of us is going to die of fright first?" She bent down to pick it up, soothing her own nerves with the kitten's motorboat purring underneath her chin.

"How did you get in here anyway? Didn't we have this conversation earlier? Miss Moon's house is for people only. Now hold tight, let me get some coffee in me, and I'll get you something to eat."

Cradling the small thing in her arm, she rounded the corner to the kitchen through the butler's pantry and froze when she realized her back door was wide open.

Rivulets of fear washed off her from the top of her head to the bottom of her toes. She couldn't remember if she had left the door open or not. She looked to the phone, but the long cord was lying on the ground, disappearing into the parlor.

Tension mounted as she tried to figure out what to do. Call the cops or run out of the house? She was thinking about making for the front door when she noticed a hastily scrawled note in Edna's handwriting.

"Forgot my purse, didn't want to wake you, snuck in through the back. Call you tomorrow!"

The note was the largest relief to Nancy's ruffled nerves.

Squawk!

She jumped at the noise. It had come from the parlor.

Forgot about that damned bird.

She backtracked into the hallway. Still clutching the kitten in one arm, she scooped up the umbrella in another. She peeked around the foyer into the parlor.

A large black bird whose wings bore bright white tips stood on the back of one of her Queen Anne chairs. Back to her, it continued its racket unabated.

Nancy scowled as she wondered if black birds were good or bad omens. Most likely bad. She would have to ask Edna about it when she got a chance.

She waved her hand at the bird from across the room. "Get on out of here. If you pooed on one of my chairs, I'll be eating blackbird pie tonight."

It didn't move or turn around. A shrill squawk filled the air in reply. The kitten in her hand bristled, digging its razor-sharp claws into her arm.

"So that's your response?" She lowered the kitten to the floor. "Go get it, Loki!"

The kitten's legs were pumping furiously before she'd even set it on the ground, reminding her of a wind-up toy car whose wheels were already spinning before it was lowered to the pavement.

The tiny kitten ran up to her Queen Anne chair and tried to jump onto the cushion, but its tiny legs couldn't reach and it slammed headfirst into the front of the seat.

Nancy stifled a laugh and pressed the button on the umbrella, springing it open and shoving it at the bird.

That got the bird's attention, and it leapt from the chair up to the curtain rod above the front windows. The kitten was close behind it, jumping and attaching itself to the age-old tapestry curtains in an attempt to climb for its breakfast.

The next ten minutes were hell for Nancy. Trying to shoo the blasted thing from her home was a balancing act between being aggressive and preventing either it, the kitten, or herself from toppling some piece of furniture or antique. After opening nearly every window and door in the house, she finally managed to get it to exit through the kitchen door into the backyard. The kitten bounded along after it.

"Don't bother coming back!"

Edna would probably be mad that the entire ordeal wasn't caught on tape and played back with Benny Hill music.

Nerves under control, she was finally able to brew some coffee.

The warm black liquid flowed past her tongue, tickling her slightly with its acidic nature. It warmed not only her mouth but continued down her throat and spread out from her chest in a fractal pattern, slowly taking over her senses. She closed her eyes and breathed in through her nose, savoring the deep, rich flavor. She was at peace for a small moment before she had to deal with the rest of the day.

"So this strapping young man is coming over tomorrow to help you clean out your attic? Robbing the cradle, aren't we?" Edna's voice was staticky over the phone, something Nancy couldn't remember it doing in at least a decade.

"I think I'll be able to control myself."

"Uh-huh."

Nancy sighed. "He'll be here most of the day. You want to come over while he's bringing down the boxes and we can go through things?"

"Count me in. After telling you to do this for so long, I wouldn't miss it. I'll bring the taquitos."

"Edna." Her voice was somber. She didn't know exactly what she was going to say. "You said you see some kind of a guru, right?"

"Nancy Codworthy Moon, are you feeling okay?"

"First off, that's not my middle name, but yes, I ... I think after seeing Linda die in my arms that night I might need to talk to someone."

Edna's tone changed immediately. Despite her playful nature and liberal use of sexual innuendos, she knew when things were serious and responded appropriately. Nancy needed both at different times, and Edna usually was correct in her decision. "Oh yeah. Guru is fantastic. She's great to talk to. You okay, Nan?"

Nancy's mind raced a mile a minute after finally admitting that she hadn't fully processed the death of Linda. She had been so focused on staying one step ahead of the emotions. Finding Peter and learning more about him seemed to fill the void, but she knew she couldn't rely on that forever. She also had other things she hadn't told Edna about yet, like the statue, which was now sitting in her roll-top desk in the library, or parts of the conversation with Linda, including the detail about dying witches.

Edna had known about the dreams since Richard left, but Nancy hadn't told her about any of the new ones. Nancy had always been a skeptic when it came to supernatural things, and she didn't want to complicate their relationship.

Right now she wanted someone to confirm she was just hearing and seeing things, not someone who would instantly attribute these things to some kind of supernatural or paranormal activity.

Still, Edna was her best friend.

Nancy squeezed the bridge of her nose. She could feel a headache coming on.

"Nan, and don't take this the wrong way, but I've been worried about you the last few days."

"Am I that obvious?"

Edna huffed. "You saw someone die in an alley after being mauled by a tiger. I'm a pretty messed-up individual, but even I have my limits. I've been holding back on you, because I know you need time to process things, but you really should go see someone. Don't wait for two years before seeking a counselor, like you did with Richard. I mean, I'm glad you and I met, but you have to admit you waited too long for that."

Nancy didn't want to admit it, but her friend was right.

"Will you go see her, please, Nan? I'll pay for the whole thing."

Nancy sighed, feeling like she was giving up something of herself, even though the whole notion was ridiculous.

"I will think about it; not quite ready to make the call yet."

"Yay!" Something bumped on the other end of the phone and Nancy heard Edna let loose a string of curse words to make a sailor blush.

Edna is Edna. No taming a wild beast.

Nancy chuckled to herself. "Have fun, but don't enjoy yourself too much."

"Noodles," Edna said through gritted teeth.

CHAPTER 9

"ELL, COME IN, COME IN. I don't bite." Nancy beckoned the boy into her house.

Peter had his hoodie pulled down, exposing his shoulder-length mane. It looked soft and warm, and Nancy resisted the urge to touch it. Younger men with long hair did look good, something she would have abhorred just a couple decades before. Suddenly Anca's petting him back when they first met made sense.

Nancy pulled a large iron key off the wall-mounted stand from the spot labeled Attic.

"So you'll never guess where this goes."

"To the attic?"

Nancy snorted. "I guess I had that coming, didn't I? Yes, you are correct, but"—Nancy put one finger beside her nose—"the trick is to know how to find the attic."

She stepped back and opened her arms wide. "You said you were impressed with the house, right? Well, prepare to be amazed. This house is really, really old. It's been around, oh I don't know, longer than I've been alive, longer than my parents would have been alive. I think mid 1850's, if I remember correctly."

She held up the key level with her face. "This ancient key isn't the only secret in the house, follow me."

She turned right from the foyer, toward the library, then another left down the hallway that led to the back rooms. She stopped at what looked like a blank wall.

Making sure Peter was watching, she put all five fingertips of her right hand onto the middle of the wallpaper-covered wall and pushed.

A seam that should not have been there suddenly appeared, forming a perfect rectangle in the wall. Behind it, blackness formed and grew as part of the wall swung inward on silent hinges.

Wooden stairs led down into the blackness, and a musty smell wafted up, stinging their nostrils. "Now I don't ever go down there, as you can smell." She waved a hand in front of her face, trying to dissipate the stench.

"Cool." Peter's eyes were wide with excitement. He stuck his head into the doorway and peered down. "Never go down there, huh?"

Nancy let go of the wall and let the door slowly close itself. "Oh never! Dreadful place. I really don't want to know what is lurking below, to be honest. The horrors of the deep are best left asleep, if you catch my drift. But you didn't come here to see the basement; you want the attic, right?"

Peter smiled faintly then pointed upstairs.

Nancy smiled back and, after a brief war in her mind over if she should say anything or not, stated, "It's good to see you smile. Let's go on the tour."

Peter followed Nancy upstairs. She pointed to the left and counted off the doors.

"My bedroom, bathroom, and another bedroom along the back wall." She turned around and gestured down to the other end of the hallway.

"Now, at the end of the hall is where we are going. Come."

Nancy hardly ever came down to this end of the hallway; there really was no reason to.

Nancy had not been up to the attic once since Richard left, and she was curious to see what was was up there. She had tried once, but the door was stuck, and what better person to get it unstuck than a strong young man?

At the end of the short hallway was a shallow cherrywood desk, ornately carved with thin spindle legs that fluted out at the bottom with claw feet. The grain was fine with a deep red stain, though not as dark as the mahogany flooring throughout the main floor downstairs, something she constantly received compliments on but had never installed herself.

"We're looking for a door like the one I showed you downstairs. See if you can find it." She took the large iron key ring from her hand and hung it on the end of a finger. She started to twirl it but quickly stopped once she remembered not only how loud it was, but also that she wasn't dexterous enough anymore to do so with such a heavy ring. She clamped down on the keys feeling older than she really was.

Peter set to work pushing on walls and squinting at corners, but nothing seemed to budge. He shrugged his shoulders and took a step back.

"No idea, ma'am."

Nancy pointedly ignored the ma'am comment. She placed the sole of her slipper on top of the claw-foot furthest from the wall, and pushed down.

The claw detached itself from the bottom of the table, rotating down, exposing a metal rod behind. An audible click signified something mechanical had changed state. She then placed her splayed fingers on the wall and pushed for a moment before releasing.

Just like with the hidden doorway below, this one seemed to melt out of the wall. Seams suddenly appeared around the door, and it sprang outward, covering up the small table.

Peter, openmouthed at the contraption, simply said, "Magic."

Behind the hidden door was another, slightly smaller door. This one wasn't covered in plaster and lath and fancy turn-of-the-century wallpaper. This door was made of solid wood, set in a frame that looked like it had been constructed two-hundred years ago, complete with hand-casted square-headed nails lovingly pounded by human hands rather than pneumatic tools. The boards were old and gray from age, dusty and drying, but everything was as solid as the day it was made.

"This is mainly why I needed you to come over. Well, this and the box lifting. I've tried to pull this door open before, but never been able to get it to budge. I was hoping you would be able to get it unstuck."

Peter looked over the doorway, through each seam. He tugged on the door a couple different ways then shrugged. "Looks like it's crooked. Do you have a crowbar?"

"I think down in the garage. Tell you what, I'll leave you to this, garage keys are on the ring by the door, and I'll make you some breakfast while you work on getting this door unstuck. Oh, and be careful. Don't want anyone getting hurt."

Peter smiled. "Not to worry; my dad had me do a lot of construction growing up. I won't hurt the house."

"I was talking about you."

Nancy turned but remembered something. She pulled some green bills from her pocket. "Oh and before I forget, here is your money."

Peter took it with a blank stare. "But I haven't finished the work. I haven't even started."

Nancy snorted. "Nonsense. My friend is coming over here soon and she and I are going to start going through the boxes that you bring down to the living room. Once you are done, then you can just leave, and I won't have to remember to pay you."

Peter still looked confused but took the money.

Nancy pointed to the upstairs portion of her house. "Now get on out of here and start earning your keep, young man." She winked and waggled her eyebrows. Peter smiled and turned.

"Oh, and Peter."

He stopped and turned back, an inquisitive look on his face.

"Be a dear and get the table in the center of the parlor moved. You'll have to pile everything right there in the center. I'll get the other chairs moved away. Oh, and scoot the loveseat back as well."

Peter gave a curt nod and took the stairs two at a time.

Nancy watched him go, wondering if she should get the figurine from the library and have it sitting on the table when he got back. "No, now's not the time, Nancy," she mumbled to herself. "Don't want to scare him off too soon."

Her mind wandered back to the night Linda died, remembering the pleading words of a dead woman. Nancy was pretty sure that Linda had meant this Peter, but what good would a jade statue do for a nineteen-year-old college kid?

She had a lot more questions, but she didn't want to burden the poor boy or back him into any corners.

She was finishing breakfast when he came down to report the unstuck door. She hurried up after him to check out the attic.

The stairs leading up were small and narrow, and given that it had been at least a decade since she had gone up these stairs, Nancy worried what she would see at the top. What had Richard been storing up here for this long? Of course she had asked him, but his answer had always been one of a shrug and a single-word response: "Books."

She thought about the basement, with its mold and mildew. She was pretty sure there had to be goblins—or worse, rats— living down there. Did crocodiles live this far north? She knew she had seen Richard take old furniture, and other stuff down there, but she had hated that place.

Peter got to the top before she did and let out a low whistle. "Man, it's dirty."

Nancy could smell the room before reaching the top of the narrow stairs.

It smelled of neglect, and timelessness. Of forgotten mementos and grandma's attic, but luckily, no mold.

A thick carpet of dust lay over everything, which Nancy expected, but what she didn't expect was everything looking so neat and organized. She had expected piles of boxes, heaped on top of each other and cobwebs filling the nooks and crannies from wall to wall.

The room was small, maybe ten feet square, with lucarne dormers looking out all four cardinal directions. The entire room consisted of wall-to-wall bookshelves, varying in height from two-feet tall where the roof slanted down at a sharp angle, to six feet in height. On these shelves was the oddest array of books she had ever seen. An eclectic mix of ancient unnamed leather-bound tomes and sixties science-fiction pulp novels, formed an alternating pattern. Leaning against them was an an old *Nancy Drew* paperback with the name torn off featuring a flapper-looking Nancy going up a staircase. She glanced back to the doorway and the stairs leading down and smirked.

Leaning up against one of the bookcases was a pile of what Nancy expected the room to be filled with. The old and yellowing boxes seemed to barely be hanging together. A few had dried glue from what was probably World War II. Some had split, allowing books and magazines from after the war to fall to the floor.

In the center of the entire room hung a single dingy bulb, suspended over a worn leather chair that faced the staircase.

A small dust-covered side table sat next to the chair and on it sat a book.

Like it's waiting for him to come back and finish where he left off.

Peter flicked on the light switch next to the stairway. To Nancy's surprise, the light bulb worked, sputtering at first then growing in luminescence. Nancy walked over to the chair in the center and picked up the book.

What was Richard reading last?

Before looking at it, she turned to Peter. "Breakfast is done; why don't you go grab something to eat while I take a look around?"

A gleam in his eyes from free food, Peter practically fell down the stairs on his way to the kitchen.

She pulled the book out from under her arm and brushed off the cover.

She read off the title in her head. She read it a second time, not believing the first.

He was reading *The Notebook.*

It was the signed first edition hardback that he had surprised her with for their twentieth anniversary. She thought she had lost that book.

Overwhelmed by emotion, she carefully placed the book back where it had been, making sure to line up the edges with the imprint of dust.

With that, Nancy turned off the light, and made her way back down the stairs, fighting back tears the whole way.

CHAPTER 10

A S PETER DOVE INTO HIS meal, Nancy decided it was
finally time to start asking questions.

"Were Linda and Anca … you know"—Nancy didn't
even want to say the word herself—"lesbians?"

Peter looked up with an odd expression on his face. He
shrugged. "I think so." He went back to eating.

"But they lived together across the alleyway from you?"

Mouth full of eggs, Peter nodded again.

Nancy waited until he had swallowed before asking her next
question.

"I was thinking about what you said about your father raising
you by himself. He must be a good man to do that, to raise you
without a mother."

"He did okay, I guess."

She paused, sucking in a slow breath to calm her nerves.

"Peter, I know it's none of my business, but if you ever need
to talk, you know you are always welcome here, okay? I guess I
worry about you. Anca seems very controlling of you is all and
… I'm sorry. I'm probably reading into this too much."

Peter nodded, very briefly.

She reached out her hand, touched his forearm, and smiled
wistfully at him.

"Forgive an old woman and her craziness."

Peter's expression was contemplative, like someone trying
to work out if they were offended or not. "Thanks for the meal,

ma'am. I really should get working on those boxes. I ... I should go."

With that statement, Peter got up and hurried upstairs.

Stupid, stupid, stupid!

Nancy cleared away the plates and loaded them into the sink for washing later. She heard Peter walking down the stairs and decided to go say one last thing before she left him alone.

He carried a large box. Dust streamed out from behind him as he stepped off the staircase and made his way down the hallway to the parlor. His face was red and puffy.

When she saw him, she lost the nerve to push him further. She decided to just apologize.

"Peter, I'm sorry if I said something to upset you. It seems like you really liked Linda. I guess finding her in the alley got to me." She paused, collecting her thoughts. "I can't get the notion out of my head that she was worried about you. She gave me something to give to you. We don't have to do it now. We can wait till after you are done. I just haven't had the nerve to give it to you yet."

Peter's face went white.

Nancy let out a nervous laugh. "My life has been different since I met Linda. Things are happening to me lately and I'm not sure how to explain them. Anyway, I just wanted to apologize for being so blunt and forward. It was wrong of me to pry into your life."

The box started to slip from his grasp, but he caught it and put it down at his feet. "She was a really nice lady. I'm sorry she died." His face was awash with so much pent-up emotion that Nancy wanted to give him a hug, but she resisted. She was already pressing him enough.

He turned back to look out to the hallway. "I should get going on more boxes." He thumbed behind him then turned and started back toward the staircase. He stopped right before the corner in the hallway and pivoted back around.

"Nancy?"

Shocked that he used her first name, she smiled and looked up at him, hands clasped together in anticipation.

"Yes?"

"Thank you for this job. It means a lot to me. I haven't had a lot of friends since I got here and, well, some people I thought were my friends turned out to just want to use me. It's nice to know that there are good people out there. I'm sorry for not telling you everything, it's just that ..."

"You barely know me?"

He shrugged. "It's not just that. It's complicated, I guess."

He turned on his heel and disappeared around the corner.

Her heart broke in two at this young man's admission. She sat down on the nearest chair as she suddenly felt lightheaded. What was going on with this young man? Why was a nineteen-year-old so troubled?

"Oh, look at this." Edna perched on the edge of Nancy's Queen Anne chair, hunched over the growing pile of boxes. She delved into the second box. Dust flew everywhere. She started coughing a bit, wincing as the dust cloud puffed into the air when she opened the box. "More books." Edna sneezed again. "I swear there has to be better way to deal with all of this. Can't you just hire a service to take it all to the dump?"

"And lose out on all this precious bonding time with my best friend? I think not. Besides, there are some good memories in these boxes."

"Really?" Edna held her head back and to the side while she delicately pulled another leather-bound tome from the box.

Nancy laughed. "You're not changing a diaper there. It's just a book."

"Yeah, book. Can you even read this? This looks like it's Russian or German or something."

"Really? You can't tell the difference between Cyrillic and Latin alphabets? Let me see that."

Edna passed over the leather-bound book. Dust swirled out into the air and Edna sneezed again. "I gotta go blow my nose, maybe take a pill or something."

Nancy smiled and took the book. It was a lot heavier than she'd expected it to be. She ran her hand over the dark cover, brushing away accumulated dust and dirt from the years of storage. Stamped into the cover was a series of characters that Nancy was having trouble pronouncing. They read, *Septuaginta Zagulajevi.* Rather than trying to sound out the words, she opened it up to look through the pages. The pages inside were brittle and yellow with age. Nancy couldn't read anything inside, but it looked Germanic to her.

She put the book down, and pulled out the next thing in the box. It was another book, but this time it was written in English. "*The Canterbury Tales.* Huh."

Edna came back in. "What's so huh?"

Nancy held up the book for her friend to see.

"Oh hey, I've heard of that book," Edna replied.

"Heard of it? You mean you haven't read it?"

Edna snorted. "Of course not, who would have read something …" She trailed off when she caught the expression on Nancy's face. "Well, I haven't had the opportunity quite yet to read it."

Nancy handed over the book. "Well, now you do."

Edna pulled her hands back. "Oh no. Not this. Can't you see this is a classic? I'm not touching that book. Besides, is it a free book in the public domain? If I really was going to read it, I'd pick it up on my e-reader."

Nancy rolled her eyes. "Those devices are just a fad. Real books will make a comeback."

"Oh, you're just a Luddite. Time to embrace the future, my dear."

This time Nancy snorted. "Not likely. I'm perfectly happy to keep reading physical books."

"Yeah, but meanwhile you're falling farther and farther behind in technology." Edna shook her head.

"Careful. If you keep rolling your eyes like that, they might get stuck."

Edna smiled. "Online dating is the way everything is going. You don't want to be stuck in a more and more digital age as someone who doesn't even own a computer, do you?"

Nancy pointed to the corner. "I have a computer."

"Yeah, I gave it to you, and how many times have you used it? I have never received an email from you."

"Well, why would I email when we can just meet up anyway? Besides, if I'd just spent my entire life on the internet we would have never met. We met face to face the first time, and I'd like to keep it that way."

Edna smiled. "Well, I agree with you there. That was one crazy summer."

Nancy grabbed a magazine from underneath a book and put it in her lap. It read *Boys Life,* had a published date of February 1961, and looked ancient, like everything else in the box.

She couldn't stop thinking that this was all Richards stuff. Things he kept in the attic, a place she never went. "I'm still mad at him, but I miss him. I just need to move on."

"You do, but you need to do it in your own schedule."

"I know, but I guess I'm not ready to do that. It's only been four years, and there were those postcards."

"That doesn't change the fact that he just disappeared on you. There is a lot of trust lost there. Even if he's alive, it doesn't change those facts. My husband at least had the decency to up and die on me."

"Edna!" Nancy put her hand over her mouth.

"Oh, don't get me wrong, I loved the man to death. But to be honest, I think our marriage was starting to fall apart anyway. Pretty sure he had a girl on the side. Anyway, it sucks, but it did end up being a good thing in the long run. You and I met, for one."

"Yes, but one grief counseling week in the woods doesn't make up for that."

"Oh, we've had a lot more than just that week. That was just the beginning, as you so love to remind me. We've have a lot more that's happened since then. Need I remind you about our little trip down south?"

"That poor horse! I promise I never meant for that poor thing to get involved."

"He was fine. Besides, I'm sure he was happy to get out of his pen." Edna winked.

Nancy couldn't help but smile. Her smile turned into a single chuckle, which turned into Edna snorting, and Nancy couldn't hold back the laughter anymore. The two abandoned all hope of progress on the book sorting while they cackled and jeered, eventually calming down.

Nancy had to wipe the tears from her eyes.

Peter entered the parlor, nodded briefly to the women, and dropped off another box.

"Oh, he is cute," Edna said after he had left.

"He's way too young, so keep your grubby little hands off the poor boy."

Edna nodded slowly, though her gaze never left him leaving the room. "I promise I'll be good."

Nancy heard a crash, followed by a thump coming from the upstairs.

She was on her feet and turning into the foyer and back toward the stairs before she even realized what she was doing.

Panic flooded her as she took in the sight on the second-floor balcony. Peter lay on his side, motionless, pushed up against the railing, which kept him from falling down the fifteen feet to the hallway below.

"Call 911!" she yelled behind her to Edna.

For the second time this week.

She rushed up the stairs as if in a dream. Panic filled her thoughts. She got to the top and took in the sight.

Two ancient, yellowed cardboard boxes lay cracked; their contents, mostly books, spilled out across the landing. A broken lamp lay on its side. The evidence of a shattered bulb was embedded in the carpet.

Peter lay on his side, back to the balusters, arms out.

At least he landed on carpet.

Nancy couldn't see any blood and the glass had landed far enough away from him that she wasn't worried about him being cut by the shards.

She watched him for a moment to make sure his chest rose and fell, which it did.

Thank God he's alive.

She stepped carefully around the broken glass toward the unconscious boy in front of her.

There was a creak behind her and she turned to see Edna, who was taking in the sight.

Edna let out a low whistle, her phone in her hand and pressed up to her breast. "They are on their way, a minute or two."

Nancy nodded and turned back to the boy. Crouching next to her fallen charge, she checked his pulse, watched the rise and fall of his chest for a moment, and inspected his head. No blood that she could see.

He was lucky.

What is it with Asians lately?

Edna sneezed behind her. "Sorry, too much—" She sneezed again and proceeded to wave her hands around in the air, trying to dispense the clouds of dust threatening to infiltrate her lungs.

"It's okay. Wait downstairs and open the door for them. I'll stay here. He should be fine."

I hope.

Nancy proceeded to pick up some of the glass closest to the fallen boy. Sirens filled the air and stopped outside her house as she dropped the last shard into a garbage can just inside her bedroom.

She stopped as she stepped out of her bedroom. Peter was on his feet, a wild look in his eyes to complement the crazy hair sticking up around him. He stood where he had fallen, his head swiveling back and forth like he was a trapped animal.

"Peter? Be careful—"

"You can't control me! I know what you're doing and I will fight it!" His eyes blazed with fury.

Nancy froze midstride, her smile fading into obscurity as she took in the frightening sight of him and the threat in his voice.

"Peter?" She fought down a sense of panic, trying to keep calm.

Peter's eyes locked on Nancy's. It must have been a trick of the light, but they almost looked golden.

He paused, his face scrunched, losing a lot of the rage it had held. His eyes darted back and forth, seemingly trying to process the scene in front of him.

"Peter, you fell coming down the stairs. Are you okay? The ambulance is on the way just in case. No one is trying to hurt you." Nancy noticed the worry in her voice even as she said it. He must have hit his head harder than she thought.

Peter's face grew dark and sinister, with a wry smile tugging on the corners of his mouth.

"I can see now." His voice was ominous, deeper than normal. His eyes went wide. He hissed and ran at her.

Nancy yelped and took a step back as he charged her, but Peter turned and took her stairs three at a time down to the first floor.

Nancy heard surprised yells coming from below as he ran outside. Edna sneezed in the distance.

Nancy, not knowing what else to do, sat down on the floor in the hallway and stared at the spot where Peter had lain. She couldn't get the image of his eyes out of her head.

He really did hiss at me. That only happens in movies, doesn't it?

She shook her head at the situation and picked herself back up off the floor when she saw Edna's head appear at the bottom of the stairs.

Better get downstairs and explain this to the poor paramedics.

"No, left on Superior."

"Are you sure?"

Nancy was developing a headache. She should have driven. Instead, she had to be a passenger to a bat out of hell named Edna.

"I've been here twice already. I know it's left."

Two more turns, and they arrived finally at the intersection that held Anca, the Chinese Theater, and Peter, who lived above.

"Park in the same spot. I need to go see if he's okay."

"He sure seemed okay when he ran past me."

"I know, but I think he was scared. He wasn't in his right mind, and I don't want Anca to find him like this."

"Anca? What are you talking about?"

Nancy didn't want to get into the whole thing with her friend. She already felt bad enough that she had been keeping so many secrets from her, but she didn't really have to time to delve into it right now.

Soon though, can't keep stringing this along by myself.

"I'll explain when I get back, but the short answer is I think Anca is abusing him."

"Abusing? Anca's like ninety years old, how could she ..." Edna trailed off when she saw the deathly serious look on Nancy's face.

"Trust me on this. I'll explain later, I promise."

Nancy shut the door to Edna's BMW a little too hard. She wasn't mad at Edna. She knew her friend lacked serious details in this matter, but she also didn't have the time to explain everything. Edna would just have to be okay with this right here, right now.

She started walking to the alleyway when a loud bang of steel on steel echoed so loud and violent that it gave her pause.

"Where is Peter?"

It was unmistakably Anca's voice, but she sounded like she was only a few feet away instead of the forty feet that it looked to Nancy's eyes. Her words had an accusatory edge to them, something Nancy didn't want to deal with right now. She just wanted to make sure Peter was okay.

She blinked, taking a tentative step back, and Anca was suddenly at the bottom of the stairs.

Nancy blinked again and considered turning to see if Edna was watching, but before she could, Anca stepped out of the shadow of the alleyway into the diminished sunlight of the early afternoon.

How did she get down here so fast?

"Where is he, witch?" Anca's thick Eastern European accent was coated in bile and poison. She was out for blood. "I know you've been filling his head with lies. Where is he?"

"I–I don't know." Nancy still couldn't believe this was happening. Where was Edna? Was she hearing all this? Anca was yelling at the top of her lungs, mere feet from Nancy, yet despite her scratchy old-woman voice, her words boomed like thunder in the open air.

Chimes rang, the door to the restaurant opened, and a couple with a small child came out, chattering in some Asian language Nancy couldn't place.

Anca glared at the family, then back to Nancy. "I better not see you around here again. You leave him alone."

Nancy finally got her wits about her. "I came here looking for *him* since he ran out of my house." Her tone was pointed but her volume low, so as not to make a scene. "I don't know what you're doing to him, but I will find out and report you to the authorities."

Anca smiled, her aged teeth seemed to be covered in some sticky residue. "We shall see about that, witch." Her eyes glanced over to the family, now standing at the bus stop about twenty feet away. "I warn you this last time. Do not come here again or I will find you. We shall see just how latent you are."

Anca turned around, took two steps back into the darkened alleyway, and was gone from sight.

Nancy blinked. "How did she do that?" she mumbled to herself.

"Wow." Edna chimed in from behind her. "You were not kidding. She's mad as hell."

Nancy turned to find her friend leaning up against the car with the driver's side door opened. Nancy sighed. She looked back down the alleyway and then glanced up at Anca's arched windows. She thought she saw a shape in the window but when she looked again it was just a shadow.

"Let's go." Nancy said. "I'll explain my theory on the way home."

Nancy was unusually tired by the time she headed to bed that night.

While she wasn't a religious sort, she almost felt like praying. She opted instead for standing on the balcony off her bedroom and watching the odd dancing lights of what had to be drunk fireflies in her backyard. It was so peaceful, so serene. How had she lived here all these years and never noticed them before? She finally decided to speak her mind into the air.

"It's been a long time, Richard. Too long, in fact. I don't want to admit it, but maybe it is time for me to move on. I hope you are okay with this. I don't know how much longer I can wait. If you're going to come back, now would be a good time."

Nancy crawled under the covers and wept into her pillow before she fell asleep.

If she had been paying attention, she might have noticed two points of reflected moonlight that watched her from the large oak tree in her backyard.

CHAPTER 11

FOLLOWING AN AFTERNOON VISITING OLD friends at the library, Nancy knew something was wrong the second she walked in her front door. Something didn't *feel* right; the hairs on her arms stood up. There was a lingering pungency like stale urine and wet hair that hung in the air. The sun would be going down in about an hour and the thought of it becoming dark so soon chilled her to her core.

"Hello?" Her voice was hesitant, cautious. She held onto the heavy oak door with one hand as she scanned around. No one was here and there was no kitten around this time.

Turning to the left, she saw that the pile of boxes looked different, taller perhaps? Fuller?

"Peter?"

She called out for him twice, but no answer.

She finally let the door swing closed and took a step into the parlor. As she walked closer, the stack of books and ancient boxes was noticeably larger, especially since Nancy and Edna hadn't even made it through one box yesterday before the entire project derailed.

Again, she called out to him, but her house was deathly silent. Despite her original trepidation, something inside of her told her that she was alone. She could feel the calm slowly spreading through her chest.

She turned around to put down her purse when she noticed something that didn't seem to fit. Under a book near the top of the newly formed pile was a bright red piece of paper.

In a sea of yellowed pages, brown leather bindings, and dust, it stood out.

She bent down and tugged on the corner. Out came a piece of artwork with a calendar on the bottom. She flipped it over to see a list of food items listed in both Chinese and English. It was a takeout menu.

Nancy recognized the name of Uncle Airo's.

The printed menu wasn't the only writing on the paper. Near the bottom, overwritten in small, neat, blocky letters was a long paragraph written in blue ink.

It wasn't any hanwdwriting she recognized.

She read through his note.

Miss Nancy,

I'm sorry that I left yesterday. I didn't realize who you were at first and I thought I was being attacked. I ran and I should not have. I'm sorry I scared you. You already paid me for the work and I didn't want to leave you without it completed, so I wanted to get it out of the way. I'm sorry for intruding. You weren't here and I already wanted to return your keys from yesterday. I put them on the key ring by the front door.

I thought about what you said and I have decided I will be leaving Madison this afternoon.

Have you ever had the feeling that your life is not your own? That somehow, something inside of you was triggered and you can never go back to being the person you thought you were? Does it terrify you as much as is does me?

My father gave me a small jade figurine when I left, told me to keep it by me at all times, that it would help me. Anca took that from me so I took something precious to her.

Thank you for being a good friend. I haven't had many since I moved here and you are the first person I've met since Linda that genuinely seems to be concerned for people rather than using them.

Thank you again for the food and the money, but most of all

*the friendship. It's good to know I'm not alone in this new world.
I will write you once I'm back in California.*

-Peter Lin

*P.S. Do not tell anyone about the book. I couldn't take it with
me, so I left it here. Please hide it and be careful. If anyone were
to find out, it would be bad.*

She re-read the letter once more, curious about what he meant
by leaving it here. She looked around the room for something
out of place but she didn't see anything that she didn't remember
being in the attic the day before. She would have to ask him
what it was and where he hid it when she wrote him.

"I will be careful, Peter; I won't tell her." Nancy turned and
looked down the hallway to the library where she knew the cat
figurine sat in a drawer.

She had planned on giving it to him yesterday after he'd finished
with the boxes, but he had bolted before she'd had the chance.

Well, once he writes me, I can mail it to him.

Nancy sat down on the loveseat, feeling a little overwhelmed.
The last few days had been a whirlwind of activity and the reality
that she had helped convince Peter to leave was a bit too much to
process while standing. She had helped him. She didn't know how
much, but she had, and even though she may never get the full story
of what was going on in his life, apparently it had been sufficient,
and that was enough for her to feel good about the situation.

She hoped he was okay. No one should be abused, especially
someone so young, and not knowing exactly how bad it had been
was getting to her in the worst way. Her mind could imagine some
pretty awful things. She had witnessed plenty being an elementary
school teacher, seeing how some parents treated their children.
The dredged up memories of past abuses and all the strange things
going on in her life lately was too much for her to handle.

At first, she fought back the tears, trying to keep her
composure despite being alone, but the emotions weighed heavy
and tears flowed down her cheeks, dripping onto her shirt.

Nancy trudged upstairs to the narrow staircase. She hesitated at the bottom of the attic stairs but finally breathed deeply and headed up. Sure enough, the entire attic was cleared out. Even the small sitting area in the center that Nancy had forgotten to mention to Peter to leave. He had swept the dust on the floor and wiped down the dormer windows to allow more light into the room.

She smiled and re-read his note. "What a nice young man." Nancy wished she knew what was going on with him so she could help. She had her suspicions but nothing concrete.

Nancy went back down to her kitchen and put on her pot of water to brew up some tea.

She was excited to delve more into Richard's old books with Edna; it felt liberating. Nancy had forgotten how much stuff one could accumulate over time.

Now she would need to get someone to help her clear out the basement.

"Yell-ow!" Despite her cheery verbiage, Nancy suspected Edna had woken from a nap to answer the phone.

"I woke you, didn't I?"

"What? No—" Edna's excuse devolved into a yawn. "Well, maybe just a little cat nap."

"Yeah, and I'm the Queen. So Peter came by and finished up the attic. The entire living room is filled with boxes. He's also heading back home to California."

Nancy read the letter to Edna, leaving out the P.S. at the bottom, since she herself didn't understand what he was talking about.

Edna let out a slow, low whistle. "I guess you were right. I would have never guessed that Anca could be doing something to that kid."

"Well, at least he's heading back home. I hope he gets the help he needs."

Nancy caught herself twirling her finger, her hand huddled to her shoulder, reminiscent of the corded phones of yore. Something out of the corner of her eye caught her attention in the pile. She looked over but didn't see anything out of the ordinary.

"I was calling to see if you wanted to come over to check out things with me."

"Oh I am so there. Let me swing by the store and grab some food and I'll bring it over. What are you up for?"

Nancy put a hand to her stomach. "Honestly? Anything but Chinese." Her mind wandered as she glanced over at the pile again, *something* was there. She felt it in her stomach as well this time, a cross between a mild stomachache and cramps.

"How about some wine?"

She forced herself to look away, back toward the butler's pantry. "I have racks of wine that I'll never drink because you keep buying more. I'll dive into the cellar and get some out."

"Roger, Roger. I'll be over soon."

After hanging up, Nancy walked into the foyer and put her hands on her hips as she looked at the nearly filled room and the narrow walkways on both sides. "By morning, I will have conquered you."

She was about to take a step toward the kitchen when her eye finally caught something out of place.

All the books and boxes were covered with a layer of dust that Nancy knew had been much worse before Peter blew them off before bringing them downstairs. But there, buried in the midst of the mound, was something that very nearly shone like the light of the moon amidst a sea of stars. How she had missed it earlier was unknown, but it was obvious now.

She walked over to the pile and picked up a couple smalls boxes strategically placed on top so as to hide what was underneath without squishing anything. She set them off to the side and looked at the book.

Nearly a foot and a half tall, and over a foot wide, the book looked positively ancient. Its thick leather cover featured an ornate carving of interwoven geometric shapes. The binding was brittle and black, like it had been charred, and among all the dusty odors of the room, she could smell the book from where she stood. The smell was nauseating, like overly-roasted pork, ammonia, and burnt hair.

She reached down and put both hands around it to hoist it up. The leather was rough on her skin, and it seemed to hum with electricity through her fingers. Her hands barely made it from the front to the back cover. She grunted with the heft of the weighty tome.

Leaning backward to help her balance, she walked to her library where the lights were on and her small writing desk lay open to use. Dust curled up in wisps as she set it down.

It was then that she noticed something else odd about the book cover. What looked like it would be an extended flap of leather wrapped around the end and seemingly melted into the book, though there was a bit of a joint where the flap disappeared, there was no indication of how to separate the two. She groaned with the effort of picking up the side so she could see better. It was like the entire cover was constructed of one solid piece of leather surrounding the entire book, preventing it from ever opening.

She put it back down and turned the light toward the book.

The ancient carvings on the front cover faded as they neared the edges. A deep-seated sense of unease came over her. This was no ordinary book, and it screamed something dark and sinister. Why was it in her house? Was this something Richard had kept upstairs? She wondered if he had more of them and glanced over at the large pile out of habit, but as she did, Peter's note grabbed her attention. The last few lines stood out to her.

"P.S. Do not tell anyone about the book. I couldn't take it with me, so I left it here. Please hide it and be careful. If anyone were to find out, it would be bad."

She looked back down at the book. It wasn't Richards, it was Peters! She re-read his entire note twice wondering if he had told her what this was and why he had brought it.

The book almost felt unworldly, and despite Nancy not believing in the occult or magic, the thought refused to dissipate. Horror flashed across her mind as she wondered if things has been even worse for him than she'd assumed. She'd thought there had been some emotional or verbal abuse, maybe even physical … but if this book was somehow involved then maybe it was something else.

She lingered on the cover, half wondering if she'd seen those markings before. They looked eerily familiar.

Had she?

Nancy grabbed a handle of the desk and yanked. Objects inside scraped and bumped with the force of the action. She reached in and took out the small jade figurine given to her by Linda a few nights before.

Her heart pounded in her chest, anticipation growing. She couldn't remember the last time she had been so excited and terrified at the same time. Her face was unnaturally warm, and she could feel her heartbeat in her temples and neck.

She turned over the jade figurine in her hand and held it under the light. She knew the characters on the face of the statue were most likely Chinese, but she had failed to recognize the ones on the bottom. The sharp lines and acute angles in the characters matched the style she now saw on the front cover of the book. They vaguely reminded her of Gaelic runes, but not quite. They were thin, with harsh angles and a violent slant to them she had never seen before in any ancient language.

She knelt down to inspect the book further. As she bent over, she saw something that caught her breath. There was a man's face on the cover of the book! It looked twisted in agony, and distorted, but it was there!

She pulled the book closer to the edge of the desk and placed the figurine on its side so the characters scratched into the soft rock faced her, and she compared.

It wasn't exact, but she decided that a few of the letterings on the bottom of the figurine were similar in shape, though not as fancily styled as the ones on the cover on the book. They reminded her of another object she had seen recently that had similar runes. She stopped, and gasped in excitement. *The bottle of wine!* She had to go look.

Lights blinked through her window and Nancy froze as she turned toward the exit of the library.

Edna! How long have I been looking at this?

A moment of panic struck Nancy, but she breathed and wondered why she was panicking about her best friend coming by the house.

She got herself up and looked at the two objects lying on her writing desk. She frowned. She shouldn't still be keeping secrets, but she didn't know what this was all about, or why this book was in her house to begin with. Besides, how strange was it that the jade cat and the book had matching runes, from a language she had never seen before?

She thought back to Peter's admonition to keep the book secret.

She needed to hide both it and the figurine from Edna, at least till she figured out what all this was about.

Outside her house she heard the car door slam shut and Edna's whistle as she walked around the car.

The wall opposite the door into the library was filled floor to ceiling with an intricately carved credenza. The bottom was lined with cabinets. The top was bookshelves. In between the shelves were pillars that separated the three sections of the case from each other. These wooden pieces were so intricately carved Nancy had wondered for years who the artist was that had made them.

But one of them housed a secret she had learned when her husband was still around. There was a hidden compartment.

Thank you, Richard.

Nancy stuck her hand underneath one of the bookcases and ran her fingers along the small grooves. She counted out to the fifth one, spread her hand, and pushed on the three closest grooves. A minute click sounded as the internal locking mechanism released, and a three-foot section of the intricate carving folded out on silent hinges. Nancy hefted the large tome from the desk to place it into the hiding spot. Like a cat being stuffed into a space that it doesn't want to go, the book seemed to resist. She wasn't able to push it through the opening, as-if some unseen barrier prevented the book from going in.

Nancy took a deep breath and tried to put the book back into the nook, but something in her head pounded.

Oh no, you don't. This is my house! You will go in!

She scrunched up her face and pushed with all her might. She was met with more resistance, like the cavity was full of Jell-O, but through perseverance and sheer impertinence, she was finally able to get the book into the space.

Finished with the book, she put the small figurine into the nook and closed the compartment just as Edna walked through the front door.

CHAPTER 12

I'M HERE!" EDNA EXTENDED HER arms in a flamboyant flair. She did love her grand entrances. She looked to the left and gasped at the massive pile of boxes. "Now that is one big pile of shit!"

"It's about time you showed up." Nancy walked out of the library. Her heart pounded and she was sure her face was flushed. "I was going to have to pour myself a glass of wine if I had to wait any longer." She didn't dare glance back, in case it was obvious she was hiding something.

Edna gave her a curious look, like she didn't fully believe her.

Nancy pulled a hair out of her face and tucked it behind her ear. She tried to smile but the action felt odd.

Edna's eyes scrunched together, then her eyebrows raised like she had come to some decision. "Well, I'm here now, woman. Let's get our drink on." Edna waddled into the kitchen to plop down the bags of fried chicken and dumplings on the island. She carried another bag of groceries in her other hand.

"What else did you get?"

"Oh, nothing, just the essentials. Now how about that wine?"

Wine. Despite hiding the book and the figurine from Edna, she wanted to check that bottle of wine to see if it had the same runes. "I think I know just the bottle."

Nancy ducked around the kitchen wall to the butler's pantry, which mostly stored wine anymore, and flicked on the light.

The small round florescent fixture illuminated with a sputter and a faint whine while it warmed up.

Nancy scanned through the bottles of wines. She couldn't find it! Did she already take it to the library? Then she remembered she had left it in the kitchen, right under Edna's nose.

She peeked around the corner from the pantry to the kitchen. Edna's back was to her, fiddling with something on the counter.

Nancy took a hesitant step inside, her mind whirling. Why was she sneaking around in her own home, behind the back of her best friend? She needed to find this out for herself first, then she would tell Edna.

She grabbed the bottle of wine when Edna turned. "Oh, that one?"

Nancy clutched it to her chest. "Oh, no, I just forgot to put this one away." She hoped her voice wasn't too nervous. She was a terrible liar, always had been. "I wanted something different for dinner." That part, at least, was true.

She ducked back around the corner to the pantry and looked at the bottle again.

The top of it was covered in wax, much like a bottle of Maker's Mark, except the wax was old and riddled with hairline cracks, and there was a distinct Chinese character stamped into the top.

She stared blankly at the label. Memories from that night flooded back into her mind as she took in the beautiful artwork, the intricate sandblasted waves etched into the glass. Her thumb rubbed over something on the bottom and she turned the bottle over.

Shining back at her in the flickering blue light of the butler's pantry were more of those runes she kept finding. She remembered seeing them back in the store but they had a lot more impact now then they did before.

Her muscles slacked and she staggered, bumping up against the countertop behind her. She nearly dropped the bottle, barely holding on to it it as it started to slip from her grasp. Panic flooded her mind. This was what she came for, but it was almost too much to process. Three objects in her house all had archaic etched characters on them. What in the bloody hell was going on?

She looked up toward the kitchen, making sure Edna wasn't watching her. Edna bustled around the kitchen, opening cupboards and grabbing plates.

She just needed answers first. Then it would all make sense.

Nancy found herself walking into the hallway from the pantry, turning to the front of the house and into the library. She stood in the doorway for a moment, teetering, her head swimming. The sun was just starting to go down, casting a long shadow in her front yard. Violet and red light poured through the top of her bay windows.

She had left her writing desk light on. She walked to it, her body on autopilot after the strange events since she had gotten home from the library.

Edna's voice humming a tune wafted in from the kitchen. Nancy turned off the light and stood in front of the bookshelf, wondering if she should hide the bottle in the secret spot in between the bookcases as well.

A car sped along the road leading up to her house, tires screeching as it rounded the corner from Gate to Humboldt, ignoring the stop sign planted there. Nancy sighed and turned her head to try to catch sight of the latest in a long line of traffic violators, but as she did so, the light from the car's headlights shined into her window, illuminating the library bookshelves.

The intricately carved sections between the shelves protruded an inch past the built-in furniture and cast a long variegated shadow against the far wall, directly above the fireplace.

Nancy's heart leapt. There was another face on the wall! It was faint and she blinked to make sure she wasn't delusional, but for a split second as the light passed over the edges of the bookcase, the same agonized face she'd seen from the book was a projection on the wall. The man's face was twisted and distorted, like he had been beaten. His mouth agape, his eyes sunken and black. The pained look on his face was something she feared she would never get out of her mind.

Nancy held the bottle and looked around, feeling like it wasn't her own home anymore. Tears flowed from her face. She didn't even know why she was crying. She felt like her world was turning upside down. She had lived in this house for forty years and she suddenly felt like a complete stranger. What was happening?

She felt alone. She wanted Richard to burst through the door and hold her, tell her it was all okay. These were just figments of her imagination, her mind playing tricks. She was tired and just needed sleep.

Some part of her knew differently. Something was amiss in her odd little world. She thought back to Peter's letter, the part about something inside of you never going back. She didn't feel comfortable in her own skin anymore, like she was split into two. The rational Nancy would have brushed this off and popped open the bottle in her hand. The panicked Nancy wanted to run. She wanted her old life back. She wanted her husband. She wanted to call her parents.

Would any of them believe her?

The sound of the wine sloshing around in the bottle drew Nancy's attention to her shaking hands. She looked down at the bottle, revulsion filling her throat. She wanted it out, gone. She put it down on the writing desk and backed up two steps, bumping against the library door. She stopped and scanned the room. Nothing jumped out at her, nothing stirred.

Cautiously, she flicked the light switch and basked in the safety that brilliance provides. Her chilled mind began to melt. She wiped her eyes and stood for another minute, watching the carvings like they would jump out at her the second she turned her back.

Get a hold of yourself, girl. You are a grown woman, for God's sake. It takes more than a couple tricks of the light to rattle you.

She ground her teeth and dug her nails into her palms, the pain steeling her senses. *Yes.* She was just overreacting. Seeing things where things didn't exist. What was that called? Nancy searched the recesses of her mind. *Pareidolia.* She knew there was a term for it.

Your mind is naturally drawn to seeing patterns and faces in things, that's all it is. Your mind is getting the better of you.

She turned around and marched back to the butler's pantry, grabbed a bottle of wine off the shelf, and strode into the kitchen. She set the bottle down on the counter harder than she expected, jolting Edna out of her reverie of cooking something in a skillet. The smell of garlic filled the air.

"Sorry about that. Got a little distracted choosing the wine." With her hand, Nancy mimicked a gun to her head. "Mind's the first to go, you know."

"Never mind that." Edna pointed with the spoon at the toaster oven. "The garlic bread is nearly done. Pop that wine open and let's get tipsy. Those boxes are calling to me to paw through them. Time to see all the skeletons you have in your closet, girl!"

An hour into her and Edna picking through the pile, with most of the first bottle of wine gone, the phone rang.

Nancy had to pause a moment after standing; the wine was getting to her, but it felt good to unwind. She'd needed this more than she'd thought.

Taking a few unsteady steps toward the phone, she answered it.

"Yellow?" She winked at Edna who smiled back.

No one spoke, though she could hear breathing.

"Hello?" Nancy asked a second time, slightly annoyed.

"Yes. Hello."

Given the thick, female European accent, Nancy knew who was calling her. Her mind grew sharper instantly. Focused.

"This is Anca."

Nancy's response was measured and slow. "I know who this is. What do you want?"

"I want to talk."

While she didn't have hard evidence that Anca had been up to no good, she felt like she needed to keep her guard up around this woman. Anca may not have been a bad person, but she sure seemed to be taking advantage of Peter, whatever that meant.

Nancy was glad that Peter had finally left. It helped her feel justified in her lack of phone etiquette.

"Look, Anca, I don't know where Peter is. I haven't seen him for a while." She glanced toward the pile in the middle of the room, feeling almost guilty for her lie. But what should she care? Anca was clearly at the center of a series of mysterious and unpalatable events and Nancy should not feel bad about lying to her.

Her voice was measured. "No fight, just talk. I know I haven't been the best type of person. I miss Linda so much. I think I grabbed first person I could to try to fill the void left by her passing. I should have never brought him into the middle."

This got a slightly interested eyebrow raise from Nancy. Anca sounded like she was reading from a script. Was this a trap? Nancy decided that somehow it was, but she wanted to know exactly when it would snap shut on her. "I would be happy to talk. How can I help you?"

"Where do you live?"

Nancy hesitated a moment before responding. "We are already talking. Does the phone not work for you?"

"Yes, I—" Anca paused. Nancy could hear noises on Anca's line. Paper's shuffling, something groaning, the tinkling of metal. "Look, I'm sorry for how I have treated you. I want to apologize in person. Clear the air. I know you think I am bad person but I'm not. I just want to explain. I miss Linda. I miss Peter. I have no one else to talk to. I'm so lonely."

Nancy's mind whirled. Did she even want to talk to Anca? Did she trust her enough to actually give her the time of day, let alone an hour of her time? She had always prided herself in finding the best in people. She should give Anca the benefit of the doubt. Maybe if Nancy could get her to open up, then she would understand more about what was going on between Anca and Peter. That might help Nancy guide Peter better once she could write to him.

Her mind wandered back to the meeting at Anca's apartment. No, she would not go back there. A neutral location would be best, for sure. Maybe with someone other than Edna. Edna's guru popped into Nancy's mind and she glanced over at her best friend, who was opening another bottle of red wine.

She thought about the note Peter had left. Maybe she should bring it with her, show it to Anca, see what she said about it. "I am willing to talk, but not at my or your house. There is a park near the library at University and Whitney. I will be waiting on a bench tomorrow at four in the afternoon. Is that okay with you? I will not be alone, do you understand?"

Muffled voices from the other side of the line, Anca seemed to have put her hand over the receiver. "I understand. Yes. Four is good. Four o'clock in the PM."

"Okay, I will see you then."

Nancy hung up and stared at the phone for a few moments, contemplating what she'd just agreed to and what she might need to do in order to prepare for the meeting. She felt like the last week of her life had been leading up this point. Something … some *force* wanted her to meet. This terrified her to her very core.

She remembered a conversation she had with her father ages ago. They were out picking huckleberries from the pasture. Little Nancy was limping from when she had dropped from the tree house in over-exuberance to pick berries with her father. As she sat in the sun, her sundress splayed out around her, she asked him if he thought faeries existed.

It took him a moment to respond, but his picking slowed for a time while he collected his thoughts. Nancy had always loved the little lines on her father's forehead when he was really thinking on something.

"I have no way of knowing, pumpkin."

She told him she thought it was a silly response and not at all what she was asking. This, of course, was a common response from her at that time. Most four-year-olds questioned everything with an insatiable appetite for knowledge. Nancy had been particularly intuitive as a young girl and knew when her father was hiding something from her. Still, he only smiled and continued picking berries as little Nancy watched the two tiny, glowing, naked people with wings flit around her hurt ankle.

Nancy had often wondered if that memory had been because she was four and apt to daydream, or if there was something to it. A few more memories tried to percolate to the surface from her distant past, but she pushed them away. She had what she needed. She knew the way forward.

Events of the last week were barreling on down the timeline without her consent. Things were in motion that Nancy could not control, and that was the problem. She'd been in control of her life, at least most of the time. It was time to take back control.

Tomorrow is going to be an interesting day.

"Truth or dare?"

Sitting on the floor beside the pile of books, Nancy chuckled, the half-full glass of wine sloshing around in her hand. Their quest for organization abandoned for reminiscing about the old days. She glanced at the three empty bottles on the side table. She wasn't even sure who had started the game of truth or dare, but she wasn't about to let Edna win.

Edna seemed like she was chewing on the inside of her mouth for a moment. "Truth."

"Okay, what age did you have your first kiss?"

Edna's face drew back with mock indignation. "Mother of Pearl, you kiss your kids with that mouth?"

"You know I don't have kids. Now spill it, girl!"

Edna was drunk. Nancy was sure of that. She made a mental note to swipe Edna's keys in case she decided to try to drive home by herself.

"Well, it was only a few years ago, if I remember."

Nancy nearly spat her wine out. She quickly swallowed and pointed her glass at her friend. "Don't start with me. Your kids are grown and gone. Come on, time to be honest. Not like anyone else here is listening."

"Susan, fifth grade."

"A girl?"

"I think she's a senator right now, actually." Edna's voice had a depth of emotion to it, almost a melancholy.

"And you two …" Nancy became suddenly embarrassed thinking about the whole situation.

Edna swept the thought away with her hand. "No, we just kissed that one time. She wanted to have a boyfriend, and of course two girls being together was pretty taboo at that age, especially in Georgia. We were on the side of the school playing hopscotch and she asked if I'd ever kissed a boy. I said no, and she said, 'Well, why don't you pretend to be a boy so I can kiss you? Then I'll pretend to be a boy and you can kiss me.' We kissed a couple times. That was it. I hadn't even hit puberty at that point, but she had. I wonder how she's doing?"

"Did you ever tell your husband that you made out with a girl?" Nancy reached for the open bottle of wine but missed in her aim. She managed to get it on the second attempt and grew sad when she realized there were only a few drops left.

"I think we're out of wine." Nancy stood. "I'm going to get some more."

Edna continued as if Nancy hadn't stood up. She wasn't even looking at her friend at this point, instead she was staring at the pile of books between them.

"I never told Bob. He was a good man, but he got very jealous of any of my exes. He only knew about Jesse, and that was only because Jesse was in prison."

"Jesse? Wasn't that your son's name?" Nancy regretted the words the second they came out. She couldn't help it; she had been too inebriated to filter her thoughts before they were released to the world.

Edna didn't seem offended. "That's where I got his name. He was the father, such that it was."

Nancy blanched. "I didn't know that, I thought…"

"Thought he was Bob's? I never told either of them otherwise. Unlikely he would have wanted to marry a pregnant girl right out of high school if I had." Edna thought for a moment before standing up.

She flashed a cheesy grin. "Enough talk about bygones, let's go get some more wine!"

Nancy.

That damned voice was back, along with flashes of blue. A dress? Gossamer flitted around at the periphery of her vision. Maybe she was drunker than she thought. She should tell Edna to find her keys. *Yes.* They would take each other's keys. Flawless plan.

The night continued as both girls swapped stories and told rude jokes to each other until Nancy found herself stumbling up the stairs.

She decided to lie down on her bed until the room stopped spinning then she would get back up.

CHAPTER 13

"NANCY MOON."

The echoing voice that had haunted her dreams for the last four years was back. Like the countless times before, the voice was that of a distant woman calling to her from another room, muffled by the plaster and lathe of aged walls.

"*Nancy Moon.*"

She was in her house, but not. The bedroom wall color was no longer a pleasant beige; it was a checkerboard wallpaper from the fifties or sixties. The furniture was the same, but something else didn't feel right about the room. Was she a little bit taller?

She walked up to the ornate hand-carved mirror perched atop her dresser.

A much younger version of Nancy stared back. Her nightgown was stark white cotton, with all but the top three buttons secure. The long sleeves that came down to her wrists and were topped with lace looked good on her.

Her face, free of the trappings of time, looked sweet and innocent. Her eyes were a brilliant green, almost luminescent in the early morning sunlight.

She smiled at her herself. She was twenty-four again, a blushing bride if ever there was one.

"*Nancy Moon.*"

She followed the voice out into the hallway, her delicate feet padding on the cold wooden planks. She would carpet them someday, but it would be years from now.

She breezed down the steps without counting. When had she started counting them? That memory seemed lost in time.

The house had always had an aged quality to it, but it was decidedly more dingy now than after she had become the mistress and caretaker of their residence. The place had needed a woman's touch.

"*Nancy Moon.*"

The voice came from around the corner, so she followed it, barely feeling the creak of the unkempt floorboards beneath her. She stopped in the hallway. Where had it come from?

She looked at the wall where the entrance to the basement lay hidden behind the wallpaper, its secret foreign to twenty-four-year-old Nancy, the only woman in the new town whose husband insisted she keep her maiden name. He'd said he liked it better than his own.

She frowned, she knew that there should be a door here, but there wasn't. Schrödinger's door, unable to be opened until it's first observed. She instead turned to the left and walked into the library.

"Hello, Nancy. So good to see you."

Linda was much younger now, nearly matching in age of the young woman in the mirror.

Nancy sat down on the chair close to the fireplace, picking up the steaming cup of tea waiting for her on a small side table.

Linda looked good, her high cheekbones and pert nose a symbol of youth and beauty. She was excruciatingly thin, even for a young Japanese girl.

"Would you like some tea?" Nancy asked, indicating the steaming china in front of her.

Linda shook her head. "You have not done what I asked, Nancy."

"But I found Peter, I told him he was forgiven." Nancy dared a glance at the hidden nook right next to where Linda sat. She didn't want to admit she hadn't given him the figurine, but somehow she felt that Linda already knew. Shame welled up, catching in her throat.

"Things are in motion, Nancy, things you cannot stop. The spark is within you if you would only embrace it. It is time to become who you were always meant to be. Peter still needs your help, but you are too busy with your own thoughts to open your eyes." Young Linda crossed her legs, the sheen of the long maroon dress she wore bounced light from the sunlight outside. Only it wasn't sunlight. There was a blackness, a void to the brightness.

"There is someone here to see you, someone who wants you to understand. I know this is difficult. You have so many questions, but Peter still needs your help."

Another Asian woman walked into the room, facing the wall. Nancy could only see one side of her as she crossed the room. Her face was different from Linda's, more round, with smaller, piercing eyes. She was taller and thicker, but still lithe. Chinese perhaps? Her eye had a haunted look to it as it stared at the wall in front of her.

She stopped just past Linda and without turning her head to Nancy said, "He needs to know I love him."

Her accent was different, more tonal, smaller perhaps, if that was possible. Terrifying in its resonance.

She took another step forward and sat down on the other chair beside Linda, turning her full body so Nancy could see.

The other half of her face was shredded, like that of Linda's in the alleyway. Mauled by a vicious beast. Strips of skin swung loosely, exposing the bloody flesh beneath.

"Please save my son," the disfigured woman pled.

"But I have."

She snapped back, vitriol coating her heavy Chinese accent. "No, you haven't. You failed in the most basic task of saving a child." The woman put her hands to her face and cried. "I just want to cradle him again, one more time. Hold him to my breast and splash tears on him. Let him feel my heartbeat once again."

She looked up, her eyes flashing gold, her voice suddenly violently dissonant. "Find him, tell him he's not a monster. Bring me to him so I may protect him."

The woman leapt off the Queen Anne chair on all fours and bounded out of the library like some loping animal.

Terrified, Nancy looked to Linda, but she was lying dead, her chest torn open as blood dripped onto the lush carpet of Nancy's library.

Nancy dropped the tea she had been holding in her hand; the hot liquid felt like penance for her sins.

Nancy bolted up in bed. Sweat dripped from her forehead and dampened the sheets. She huffed, breathing in, feeling the bite of air in her lungs. She felt alive again. Real. Present. Older.

She looked down at the nightgown she wore; it was old, yellowed, and threadbare. The same one she had worn in the dream, only drastically aged from many decades of wear.

"I need a new nightgown," she gasped to herself in between pulls of air.

She looked around the room. Everything was back to normal. The tacky 1950s wallpaper was replaced with a pleasant beige color. The furniture, handed down for generations through her husband's family, carved untold decades before, remained, looking slightly more worn in the last forty years than it had in the dream.

It had felt so real, though, so vibrant.

She lay back down and closed her eyes, hoping the headache from too many bottles of wine would dissipate, when she smelled something dark and bold coming up from the kitchen downstairs.

She followed the scent, drawn by the allure of a percolating cup of coffee, her mind swimming in the miasma of lingering sleepiness and the confusion brought on by terrifying visions.

What did it all mean? Who was the woman with the shredded face? Was she Peter's mother? Peter had said that his mother had died when he was too young to remember. That was the only thing Nancy knew about her. Why would her mind torment herself with images of a woman she never knew? She shuddered, a chill crawling down her spine.

"Good morning!" Edna was far too chipper for a morning like today and had Nancy sitting and supplied with a steaming cup of black coffee in no time. "Well, you look like something the cat drug in."

Nancy couldn't help the involuntary glance at the backdoor, wondering where the small feline was. It had disappeared a couple days ago, after chasing the bird out the back door. Hopefully it would show up soon.

The dream present in her mind, Nancy wanted to talk to Edna, to tell her what was going on and fill her in on all the small things she hadn't mentioned to this point. It tore at her that she was keeping things from her best friend.

What had that woman said to her? That Peter wasn't safe? How could she know? How would Nancy know, since they were a product of her dreams? Had he left some kind of clue to his whereabouts?

Her heart sank when she looked up and saw that the note Peter had left her was still sitting on the counter, not two feet from the coffee pot.

She glanced to Edna. Even through the haze of drinking, she remembered the look on Edna's face the night before. It was rare for Edna to bring up all the lost men in her life and Nancy had been too pre-occupied with getting more wine to engage.

"I'm sorry," was all Nancy could say.

Edna Maddox had woken up that morning with a wicked hangover. As much as she'd wanted to stay lying in the bed of Nancy's guest room, she need to piss something fierce.

By the time she tromped down to the hallway bathroom and taken care of Mother Nature's urgings, it was too late to go back to bed.

"That woman is going to be the death of me." She tried to fix her hair as much as she could, but without her brushes she wouldn't have much of a go of it. Nancy only kept a small plastic comb down here and Edna had forgotten to bring her travel bag the night before.

Hair somewhat under control, she padded out to the early morning light and made her way into Nancy's kitchen. "I swear that woman doesn't belong in this century."

Nancy's coffee maker was so old that Enda jokingly called it World War II surplus equipment. She knew it wasn't quite that old, but it was still probably from the eighties.

She fired off the old machine and wandered into the parlor while it spurted and sputtered behind her.

Despite the overabundance of alcohol consumed the night before, they had made pretty amazing headway on the pile and would most likely need just an hour or so to finish it up this morning.

Edna casually picked up an old, worn paperback of *Great Expectations* before sneering her nose at it and dropping it into the donate pile.

"Save her from herself."

She glanced out the front window, noting an old Ford pickup in the driveway of the house across the street. "Huh, Nancy been holding out on me?" She hadn't seen the truck before and Nancy hadn't mentioned anything about someone moving in.

She smirked. Pickups usually meant men, particularly the rugged outdoorsy types. She waited a little longer to see if she could see any movement but eventually gave up to go pour herself a cuppa.

She was about halfway through with her first cup when she noticed a red paper on the counter. Curious, she picked it up. It looked like a Chinese takeout menu, but on the back was scrawled a letter from Peter.

She finished the letter and rubbed at the twitchy eye she got when something was bothering her. Nancy was a dear, but she had clearly been holding out on her.

She knew what Nancy needed, really needed, was not her. It was someone far wiser and more astute at these things. A vague memory from the haze of last night wormed its way into her head. Oh yes. YES! Nancy had made the call. She had scheduled an appointment. Life was about to get way more interesting.

She didn't have to wait long for Nancy to wake up, come down the stairs, and stumble into the kitchen haggard and half-asleep.

"I'm sorry," Nancy finally said.

"What's that?" Edna looked up from her newspaper and gave Nancy a half-hearted glance before going back to her reading.

"Edna." Nancy paused, fingering the lip of her coffee mug like she did when she was trying to figure out what to say.

Edna met her gaze and turned sideways to glance at the paper on the counter. "That? I already read it."

Nancy sighed. "I know I …"

"I know what you need," Edna stated, folding the newspaper in her hands.

"What's that?"

"I think you need to see Ushageeta."

"Usha what?"

"Ushageeta? Remember, my life coach?"

Nancy's eyes narrowed. "She's your life coach now? I thought last time we talked about her she was a guru or sherpa-something helping you on your spiritual journey."

Edna dismissed her question with a wave of her hand, tossing the folded paper onto the middle of the island. She couldn't remember how many times she had tried to get her friend to see someone, anyone, about talking things out, but getting Nancy to consider paying someone to talk was like pulling teeth. Ushageeta was fantastic, and if what Edna suspected was going on with Nancy was even half true, then Ushageeta would be the best and possibly only person Nancy should see.

Edna knew a shaman in Canada, but Ushageeta was it for miles.

"Hon, something is going on with you. It's plain as day, and I don't want to pry, but you seem to have something you need to get off your chest. If you're not going to talk to me, *your best friend,* about it, will you at least talk to a trusted advisor?"

"Now she's an advisor?" Nancy looked frustrated.

"Sweetie, I know you have a lot on your mind lately. I just want you to be okay, but something big is going on and you won't talk to me."

Nancy slumped, nearly spilling her coffee with the sudden motion. "Is it that obvious?"

Edna cleared her throat. "First, you've been dodgy and subversive since you found Linda in the alleyway. I've already said you should talk to a counselor about it."

"But I ..."

"Can I continue?" Edna voice was heated. Her volume tended to rise with her mood and how excited she was about a certain topic. She knew Nancy would forgive her for her boisterous attitude.

Nancy smiled apologetically. "Of course, I'm sorry."

"Second, I've never seen you agree so fast to going to visit supposed drug dealers in the middle of the night. That alone should send you to the psychiatrist for an evaluation. But above that was what you wouldn't stop talking about last night."

Nancy stared in silence for a moment, her face looking like she was either constipated or trying to puzzle something out. She glanced to the counter where the four empties from last night sat.

"What did I say?"

Edna smiled. "You kept saying you wanted to go see Ushageeta."

Nancy laughed dismissivly. "I what?"

"Oh yeah, you leaned in at least three times to me and said, 'Psst, I have a secret, and I need to talk to Usha about it.' I tried to get you to tell me, but you kept saying not to tell Edna but then refused to tell me. I believe at some point you called me Christine?"

Nancy blushed. "To tell you the truth, I have been thinking about it."

"Well, you did more than think about it. You called her around one in the morning and set up an appointment."

"Oh my God. I did what?" Nancy stood off her stool in stark surprise. "Please tell me I didn't."

Edna turned around, stretching from where she sat to grab the note from Peter off the counter and hold it out for Nancy to take.

Nancy held the paper in her hand, reading her neat handwriting scrawled across the menu. *Ushageeta 4pm.*

"Why is *this* here?"

Nancy held out the paper, pointing at a spot where Peter's name was written half a dozen times, once with a heart traced around it.

Edna felt her face flush with heat. "Oh, that one may have been me," she admitted. "He was pretty cute, you have to admit."

CHAPTER 14

"THIS IS HER HOUSE?"

Nancy hopped out of the car and took a couple steps up the walkway while she waited on Edna to catch up. Edna took the lead up to the house.

From the street, the house looked run down. Typical midforties stucco-covered ranch house with a single vacant carport. Getting closer though, the house appeared to change. What seemed like a pile of trash from the distance in the waning sunlight of the afternoon now was a small clump of garden gnomes all working to dig a hole in the ground.

Nancy chuckled to herself as she looked at the chubby little guys with their floppy hats. She'd never seen them cast in such a way as to be in the middle of working. Usually they just stood there holding on to a shovel with a dopey grin on their face.

Flowers and rocks dotted the small front yard. It looked like a pleasant meadow, once she observed closer.

Despite the age of the house, it seemed to be in good repair. The stucco was largely free of cracks, and the mustard-yellow paint that looked atrocious from the street was much better close up.

The front door was a dark, small-grained wood with an odd sigil carved into it spanning nearly the entire door. The circle contained smaller circles inside of it, forming a triangle. It reminded Nancy of the Spirograph drawings she used to make as a teenager. She wanted to touch it but pulled her finger back as a shadow passed across the front window before the door opened.

A young Indian woman, hardly more than a girl, looked out from the doorway. She eyed Nancy up and down for a moment before setting her gaze on Edna. "Miss Edna, welcome. Come in." She had a petite melodic Indian accent that matched her small nose, and large, inquisitive brown eyes. Her long brown hair hung to the small of her back and seemed to sparkle in the afternoon light.

Edna smiled and nodded, then slipped her shoes off before stepping into the house.

Nancy breathed a sigh of relief that her sneakers were a little on the loose side, and she slipped them off without untying anything. The girl held open the door for her with a curt smile as Nancy pulled off her shoes.

Stepping inside felt like traveling to a completely new world separated by space and time from the one she knew. The strange feeling, the sensation of a slight tug on her skin as she crossed the threshold, mirrored her experience in Anca's apartment days before.

Harsh opposing neon pinks and forest greens dominated the palate and gave Nancy a sense of apprehension. Just like Anca's home, the smell was overpowering. Unlike Anca's apartment, however, this home was far more organized. No piles of books and papers covering the neatly arranged furniture. While filled with numerous curios and books, the shelves were organized, with a sense that this home was lived in, rather than a dumping ground for the days detritus.

"The Mother will be with you shortly," the younger girl stated in a flat dull tone.

"Namaste." Edna put her hands together and bowed slightly. The girl gave a curt little nod of recognition before turning. Nancy noticed the start of an eye roll as the girl turned away from Edna.

Nancy smiled.

Edna sat down on the couch underneath the dingy front window. "Well, what do you think? I don't like curry, but the smell in this house, with this getup. Oh, I love it."

The creak of rusty metal caused Nancy to turn to see the young woman wheeling in a positively ancient looking woman. She must have been at least a hundred years old if she was a day. Her darkened shriveled skin hung off her delicate frame. She was so skinny that it was as if she hadn't eaten in a month.

"Guru!" Edna squealed.

The old woman grimaced. She pointedly avoided Nancy and instead looked at Edna.

Her gaze was downright piercing with a hint of something behind those eyes that Nancy could only describe as immense prescience, something she had remembered seeing in Anca.

Despite the woman's aged look, Nancy got the impression that she was positively dangerous. Nancy's sense of caution skyrocketed instantly, causing her hands to become moist with sweat.

"Sit already. I'm not going to get up for you," the old woman croaked. It was the voice of someone who had lived a couple lifetimes surrounded by cigarettes—hoarse, scratchy, and driving. Nancy wanted to turn and leave, but despite her will, her muscles refused to obey.

"Sit," the woman commanded again.

Nancy sat.

Ushageeta raised her head slightly to address the young girl that seemed to be her caretaker. "You can leave us."

The girl gave a small curtsey and filed out of the room.

"What was so important that I had to get woken up at the shit end of midnight?" She continued to address only Edna, hadn't so much as flicked her eyes in Nancy's direction.

Edna replied, "It's actually only four in the—"

Ushageeta cut her off. "I know what time it is right now. I'm referring to getting woken up in the middle of the night by a drunk latent." She remained locked onto Edna.

Nancy noticed something strange about the woman's eyes. It was like electricity was coming off them, little tiny bright blue sparks danced across the surface of her dark brown and bloodshot eyes. Nancy blinked, and the sparks where gone. She blinked twice more, realizing just how bad her eyes were playing tricks on her in the evening light.

Nancy could do nothing but stare openmouthed at the old woman. Everything about this situation was screaming for her to get up, grab Edna, and leave. None of her muscles would so much as twitch in response, despite her inner mind screaming at her to do so.

Nancy realized Edna hadn't said a word in response. Nancy turned to look at her friend, amazed that her head still worked, but Edna wasn't moving. She sat on the couch next to her, hands clasped in her lap, mouth half open as if she was ready to spout off some new quip, but her eyes were out of focus and hollow, like the lights had been flicked off and she was hypnotized, sitting there slack-jawed, awaiting a command to turn her into a chicken.

Terror mounting in her mind, Nancy turned slightly back toward Ushageeta, expecting her to still have her eyes locked on Edna, but they weren't.

Ushageeta's searing eyes lay completely focused on hers. "Hello, Nancy Moon. So nice of you to come into my home."

Nancy couldn't move. Her mind halted. She tried to turn back to her friend, to see if Edna's frozen state was just a figment of her imagination, but Nancy found she couldn't so much as flex her jaw.

Ushageeta pulled up a bony arm with dripping brown wrinkled skin and raised it to Nancy's forehead.

Nancy didn't know what she should do or if she could do anything at all. What the hell was going on?

The woman wheeled herself closer, placed her thumb in the middle of Nancy's forehead, and spread out her bony fingers over the top of her head, pressing forcefully. Her fingers were abnormally warm to the touch, and continued to grow in heat. Her breath was starkly sour and pungent. Nancy wanted to cringe, to shy away but sat there unable to move.

"Edna didn't tell me you were a latent. Oh what fun this is. Why did you come here?"

Nancy wanted to respond, wanted to scream, cry, yell, throw things, and run away, but she wasn't able to move or even think clearly. The warmth spread from the woman's fingers into her head, filling her cranium with a heat that was almost unbearable before a coldness seeped in to take the edge off. The warmth seemed to mingle with the cold in a spiral of power that proceeded from her head down her spine and out into her extremities. Her fingers and toes, even the three on her right foot that hadn't had feeling in years suddenly became alive with activity.

All at once the heat was gone. Ushageeta was sitting back in her wheelchair with a wide grin plastered on her face. The half a dozen missing teeth seemed appropriate for this woman.

The terror she had just had moments before abated. She was back. She was present. She could move.

"So you don't know, do you?"

Nancy wanted to turn, look at her friend, wake up Edna and leave, but she felt compelled to answer.

"Um, know what?"

Ushageeta folded her hands in her lap, pulling the blanket closer while she shook slightly. "I do apologize for that little show. You have probably never had it done to you, but I had to know why you were here."

"What did you do to me? What did you do to Edna?"

The old crone shrugged and smiled again as she nodded her head at Edna. "I'll tell you how I did it if you answer my questions to my satisfaction." Ushageeta smiled again, the grin seeming to be wider than a Cheshire cat's. "Oh deary, you have so much to learn about so many things. My little look into your mind told me that you have a lot of questions."

She rearranged the blanket again and looked back up at Nancy, her dark brown eyes somehow softer with a hint of yellow or gold.

No longer did she seem to be a scary woman. She just looked like a frail centennial in a wheelchair fit for someone twice her size.

Nancy looked over to Edna, who still sat in the dazed stupor, as if in suspended animation.

"Oh, don't worry about her. She's fine. Call it … hypnotism, if you will. I just felt like you would be more willing to discuss things if she wasn't listening."

Nancy swallowed. It was too true. Despite her reticence to talk to a complete stranger, somehow that was better than talking to her best friend. At least she could leave here and never see Ushageeta again.

Nancy felt defeated even though she didn't know she had been in a war. Like a battle had just taken place without her knowing. She swallowed and tried to clear her mind.

"Can I ask you to unfreeze Edna? She needs to hear this as much as you, probably more so."

This seemed to please the old lady. "I like that. Tenacity and putting others first. Those are good things to have." She snapped her fingers and Nancy heard Edna's exasperated breath behind her.

"So spill it," said Ushageeta. "I don't have all day."

CHAPTER 15

NANCY LAID OUT HER STORY to Ushageeta. She started with the tiger on the car, finding Linda in the alleyway, along with her request to find someone named Peter and give him a message and a jade figurine. She tried to tell everything word for word as well as she could remember it.

Ushageeta tended to nod along and agree with a grunt most of the time, but she did ask for clarification and more details about when Peter had passed out, including the things he had said. Ushageeta was also very keen on knowing Edna's reaction to the whole scenario, something Nancy also did while glancing occasionally at her friend.

Through it all, Edna remained silent as a mouse, nodding along with a gleam in her eye. Nancy knew it was probably killing her to stay silent.

After mentioning the note Peter had left her, Nancy was about to bring up the book but stopped herself before she did, remembering Peter's request that she not share her knowledge of the book with anyone else. She decided, for sake of trust with him and because she didn't fully understand the book's purpose, to leave it out.

Edna had already read the note, but didn't know what it was referring to, much like herself before she found the book.

Thinking about the note made her think of Anca, and how she had missed their meeting.

"Something on your mind?" Ushageeta asked.

"No, uh, I just realized that I missed an appointment with someone this afternoon." She didn't want to admit that it was Anca, but the meeting had not crossed Nancy's mind all day after the events of the dream and this morning with Edna.

She concluded with as many details as she could about the dream, from meeting a younger Linda, to the Chinese woman who she was increasingly convinced was Peter's mother. She even told Ushageeta her suspicions that somehow Peter still wasn't safe and that she had failed as his protector.

Her story all told, Nancy sat back, wishing she suddenly had a cup of tea or something stronger to drink. Her mouth was parched. Her mind was clean, or was it simply more weighed down now that she had reconstructed all the oddities in her life over the last week? Either way, she felt like she could think clearly now.

She worried what Ushageeta would say about this. Nancy was prepared to listen, however. Edna was right, lot of strange things had been happening and she would take answers from just about anyone at this point.

Ushageeta sat back in her wheelchair, her intertwined, emaciated fingers tapped her pursed lips repeatedly while she hummed to herself, like she was carrying on a conversation in her mind of which only the deepest notes were vocalized and wafting through her chest.

"Well, it is a lot to think about, is it not?" She turned her head slightly to Nancy's left. "What do you think, Edna?"

Nancy turned her head. Edna was sitting there in a similar leaned-back position. Her hands were folded in her lap and she looked calm but alert.

Nancy opened her mouth to say something but nothing came out. What was she going to say? Why had she withheld this from her for so long?

"I'm so sorry, Edna. I should have told you earlier about all this stuff. You were right. I need to not bottle things up like I tend to do."

Nancy braced for a retort but all she got was a smile. "It's okay. I knew that you were struggling with things, and I know how hard it is for you to open up. I only wanted you to be able to say what you wanted without fear of my opinion or judgment. I'm confident Guru will be able to help you."

Edna put a comforting arm around Nancy's shoulders before continuing. "I'm glad you were able to get it out." She turned to the old woman in the wheelchair. "So what now?"

Ushageeta was still tapping her lips with the tips of her paired-up index fingers. She stopped tapping and frowned.

"There are many things going on here, and some of it I'm not prepared to discuss with you quite yet. I will need to consult with others on it before providing you with an answer, but what I can tell you is this."

She put her hands on her knees and leaned forward. The brightly colored yellow and red blanket that seemed to be the only thing keeping this frail woman from freezing to death fell off her shoulders, and Nancy resisted the urge to get up to put it back.

"Anca Petran is a dangerous individual. You were right to be concerned about her and this Peter boy. I can't tell you if he is safe. You said he was taking a bus back to his family, is that correct?" Nancy nodded, which Usahgeeta echoed. "Then there is not much you can do about him now. Hopefully, he will reply once he has arrived and will be able to fill you in on his situation."

She leaned back a little bit more and folded her arms across her chest. "As for the dreams, I cannot say. Dreams are a strange thing. Sometimes they are simply the mind trying to process all the detritus we deal with as humans, other times the spirits beyond the veil may try to use that avenue to communicate with us."

Nancy spoke up. "So it could be Linda trying to talk to me?" Half of her thought it was ridiculous that she was even taking the notion seriously, but after the last week, Nancy was starting to wonder about her own sanity.

"Or it could just be a guilty old lady who is feeling bad that she didn't watch the boy she was trying to help actually get on the bus," Ushageeta stated, shrugging her shoulders.

Nancy was impressed with the woman's insight. She half expected Ushageeta to blame it all on some mystical mumbo jumbo, but guilt was a insightful notion. Still, Nancy was more inclined to believe that it really was Linda's ghost. Nancy became aware that Ushageeta may have intuited that from her, or from Edna explaining about her friend, and thus phrased the answer as such to help build trust.

She didn't know how to feel about that; it could either be endearing, or creepy.

"The important thing is that I know Anca, and I know she is dangerous," Ushageeta continued.

"How do you know her?" Edna queried.

"She and I run in some of the same circles. I knew Linda Hamada. She was an amazing woman. So kind. She sold herbs, I sell palm readings." She nodded at Edna, the corners of her mouth twitching up slightly. "Or in her case, I milk her for all the money I can get."

She winked at Edna, who smiled back with a big dopey grin.

"I can't answer all the actual questions you have, but yes, I saw them all in your mind. The spark, the eyes. You are not crazy. You are latent. I can't go into it all right now, but you have a power inside of you that has not manifested until now. Maybe it was the shock of finding Linda in the alleyway, maybe it's the alignment of the moon and stars. I cannot tell without further investigation, but your dreams are not just yours alone. They are real, and you are being called upon from beyond the grave."

Nancy's mind reeled. What was she talking about? Eyes? Did Ushageeta mean the golden eyes she'd been seeing lately in various people, including her?

Next to her, Edna made a noise that reminded Nancy of a kid who just couldn't contain their excitement but knew she wasn't in a place to express it the way she wanted. Edna was ready to explode. Ushageeta had just told Nancy she had powers. She needed to know more.

"Power, like magic?"

"Yes, magic." She paused, tapping a fingernail on the metal frame of her wheelchair for a moment before leaning forward. Her eyes had that dancing electricity she had seen earlier. "What do you see in my eyes?"

Nancy swallowed, was she ready for this? Did Ushageeta mean to call her out on the fact that she saw the sparks? Nancy suddenly felt very small and very young. It was like hormone-driven puberty all over again.

"I see little lightning bolts in your eyes."

Ushageeta smiled then gave a small nod to Edna, whose own eyes looked like they wanted to burst out of her skull.

"Nancy Moon, you have something inside of you that has been dormant for far too long. You are a witch, and you lack instruction." She leaned back again in her wheelchair, the sparks in her eyes gone. "Again, I don't have time now to get into it, but you are special and I will have to schedule some time to help you understand the world around you."

Nancy heard a humming sound and looked to the side for its origin.

Nancy smiled at her friend. "You okay, Edna?

Edna nodded furiously. Her tightly curled hair bounced as she rocked back and forth on the couch. Finally Edna couldn't contain it any longer. "My best friend is a witch!"

Then Edna was on her, hugging, crying, laughing. The two shared a cathartic moment together now that everything, or at least most of everything, was out in the open. Nancy suddenly felt drained, and wanted to get home.

"I think it's time to go. I want to lie down."

Edna seemed confused. She glanced at Ushageeta and seeing the earnest look in the old woman's eyes, agreed. "Of course, let's get you home."

Nancy stood then bent over to shake Ushageeta's hand. "Thank you for your advice." She started to turn then stopped. "Guru," she added.

Edna snickered behind her.

No words were shared between them as they left Ushageeta's home and loaded into Edna's car. They drove in relative silence, only breaking it with small talk and chitchat about the state of the buildings.

Everything, well nearly everything, was out on the table now. Nancy didn't know if they needed to discuss this into the ground or if it was best to let it sit for a while. Either way seemed wrong, but also right.

Saying there were butterflies in her stomach was a gross understatement. It felt like a den of moles had setup shop in there and were busy remodeling the place just in time for guests.

No other cars stirred on Nancy's street as they drove up and parked.

Edna finally broke the excruciating silence. "You okay?"

Nancy shook her head. Her mind wouldn't stop working, refused to calm down. She didn't want to believe she was a witch. It was too much to process. She needed a night off to think through things.

Edna seemed to read her mind. "We don't need to talk. We really don't. Today's been a, well, interesting day. I think it needs time to soak in. More of that wine is in order, don't you think?"

Nancy felt like she was going over the edge. If she was a witch, did that mean her parents were too? Should she call and ask them? She would have to re-think certain things. Did she need to attend meetings? Would she need to stock her cabinets with eye of newt and wing of bat? Where would one even find that?

She knew she was losing it and refocused on her friend who had been so nice about it all. "You always know what to say."

They ventured inside and Nancy made tea. As she filled the teapot and put it on the burner, she couldn't help but glance in the direction of the library, thinking about the book.

Everything else had been brought up today, but why had she held back on that? She felt like she needed to finally come completely clean with Edna. She deserved it, and Nancy needed to move past this hiding of the truth. Not telling Ushageeta about the book was one thing, but Edna was her friend, and she deserved to know.

"I have one more thing I need to show you, in the library. I didn't bring it up with Ushageeta because, well, I haven't been able to really figure it out myself yet." She stole a glance outside, noting the lack of sunlight. That was perfect. Maybe a car would pass by and Edna could see the same face. "But given everything else, I haven't been able to get it out of my mind."

Nancy grabbed two cups and placed them on the counter before placing a teabag in each. "We have a couple minutes till the water is boiling."

Nancy led the way to the library where she flipped on the light. The second she walked into the room, she felt a chill run up her spine, culminating in her head. She stopped and shuddered. She put out her hand to steady herself.

"You alright?" Edna's face grew concerned.

"Yeah, just got the willies is all."

Edna frowned. "Well, don't faint on me, I probably wouldn't be able to pick you up."

Nancy chuckled slightly as she held onto the doorframe to help balance her. "You mean you wouldn't have that superhuman strength I hear about?"

Edna smiled. "Pretty sure that only works with mothers when their children are trapped under cars. Besides, I'm certain you're the mother in this relationship."

"If that's the case, I have a few decades of spankings I need to catch up on."

Edna winked. "You would be the type, wouldn't you?"

Nancy recoiled. "Oh you. I didn't mean it like that."

Edna laughed. "Of course you didn't, which is why it's so much cuter when you overreact." Edna grabbed Nancy around the shoulders and squeezed. "Feeling better?"

Nancy nodded. "Yeah, just one of those spine tingling things. Been a long day I think. I'll be glad to get some sleep."

Nancy took a couple steps forward and turned. "I told you my husband inherited this house from his uncle when he passed away. Richard used to hide our valuables behind this spot in the library."

Edna clapped her hands and giggled with delight. "Such excitement!"

Nancy breathed in slowly, calming herself. When the tingle drew up her spine again, she shuddered, twisting her head slightly to the sensation as she breathed out. A feeling warmed over her; it was like she could feel someone at the door. X-ray vision without the sight. Women's intuition on steroids. She had the strong sense that two people were at the door, maybe three? Clearly she needed some training on these new witchy powers of hers.

Nancy took a step forward toward the hidden compartment when the doorbell rang.

CHAPTER 16

NANCY MOON.

Nancy recognized the voice in her head immediately. It was the girl in her dream. The one in the blue dress.

"Who could that be?" Edna asked.

Nancy shook the dream voice out of her head before replying, "I'm not sure."

"Should I answer it for you?" Edna started walking toward the foyer.

Be careful.

The voice in her head called to her again.

"No, I'll get it. Stay here."

Nancy walked out of the library and over to the front door. A forceful knock surprised her again as she grabbed the handle. She breathed again. Calming herself, then opened the door.

Who she saw shouldn't have been a surprise, yet somehow she already knew.

"Anca." She looked back and forth through the door to look for the others that she felt. Nancy didn't see anyone, which was disconcerting with the feeling she had. "What brings you here this late?" *And how did you know my address?*

Anca looked up at her, her eyes fuming. "I go to park and you not there. Why you not there when I come?"

"I am sorry, Anca. Something else came up and I was not able to make it to the park."

Anca pursed her lips before talking again. "You break

promise of meeting. I have to track you down."

Nancy frowned at this statement. "I'm sorry, but I had something come up. I realize I made an appointment with you, but I'm not going to take this accusatory tone from you. It's late. I'm about to go to bed. If you still want to talk about Linda, I will be happy to discuss it tomorrow or the next day. I'm tired, and I am sorry you made the drive all the way out here for nothing, but I have to insist that we do this tomorrow."

Anca took a step forward, the edge of her shoe just barely touching the threshold between the brick of the porch and the wood floor of the foyer.

Nancy heard the voice in her head again. *Shut the door, Nancy. Drive the witch from your home.*

Anca looked up in surprise at Nancy. "What did you say about me?"

Nancy responded. "I didn't say anything. Now please if you could just —"

Anca took another step forward but stopped, as if some invisible wall was in the way.

Nancy remembered the feelings she had when she entered Ushageeta's and Anca's homes.

Anca took a step back, shaking her head slightly as she muttered something so quiet Nancy couldn't pick it out.

Nancy tried to fill the silence. "I'm really sorry about not being there. Something came up that I couldn't miss."

A mixture of emotions flashed across Anca's face. She looked away for half a second. A tear flowed down her cheek. "No. I'm sorry for way I treat you. I have had rough week, and I think I was in shock over Linda's death. I see that now, I see that I've not been treating her death like I should and the main reason I wanted to see you tonight was to apologize. I also treated you poorly when you came looking for him after he … he disappeared."

Nancy didn't quite know what to say. Anca seemed genuinely remorseful about Linda's untimely death. People grieved in different ways, didn't they? Maybe Anca was just unable to process the fact that Linda was dead until now? Something tugged at Nancy's mind, though, telling her this was not a good idea. Was it? Would it really make much of a difference? She had a lot to think about and a long and confusing day to process. Still, having Edna here meant the two would be up late talking about things anyway. Edna didn't seem to know how to go to bed before midnight.

She glanced over to look at her friend, but Edna wasn't where she had originally been standing. Maybe she had gone to the kitchen?

She looked back at Anca, who had another tear flowing down her cheek. She looked like she had lost a hundred years of age. Nancy's heart dropped. Something seemed amiss, but it was all so confusing. She felt a slight tingle in her stomach.

"I'm sorry, Anca. I'm really tired. I was about to go to bed myself. Can this wait till tomorrow?" Nancy had the flash of a second—or was it third?—presence in the front yard. She looked past Anca but didn't see anything. She wondered if Edna had snuck out the back door to get to her car.

"Please, I came to give you a gift. I only need to be here for a minute then I will leave and we can meet another day." Anca smiled and that was too much for Nancy. Her normal logical self was being taken over by her emotional side, something that didn't react too well to logical explanations.

"May I come in?"

Be careful. That voice again, only much more distant this time.

She nodded, managing a weak smile. "Fine. Just for a minute." Nancy took a step back to allow Anca to come in.

The second Anca crossed the threshold, Edna, who seemed to be hiding in the library, sneezed. It was enough to knock Nancy out of the emotional haze that clouded her judgment. Reality slammed into her like a derailed train, chaos and death, despair and terror all hit her at once. Her mind flashed back to the last few times Edna had sneezed and something clicked. *The tiger!*

In that singular moment, Nancy realized a key piece of information she had been missing this entire time. It all was so fantastic, but after everything that happened, was it really that out of the question?

Anca's face was a sneer and a laugh, twisted in joy and disdain, with a hint of triumph.

Behind Anca came a roar and a wall of orange and black fur filled the doorway. *Oh God, what have I done?* Nancy's hunch was correct.

Nancy stumbled back from the door, hitting her head on the wall behind her.

The snarling beast bounded into the foyer, filling up most of the space. Anca squeezed in behind it, shoving the cat's hindquarters out of the way so she could get inside. Nancy seemed to be seeing stars, but she recognized something in those terrible feline eyes, something she had seen before.

"I thought I noticed something about you before." Anca's voice had changed, no longer mournful and sad, but willful, powerful. It was the same voice she used when she was angry.

Anca took another step forward as Nancy took a step back. Nancy kept a pistol upstairs in the side table next to her bed, but she doubted she would be able to make it up there in time.

Anca snapped her head to the side and looked down the hall to the library where Edna was standing. "Very clever, putting a nullicant on your house. Such a powerful one, too. You have been hiding out on me, haven't you? Oh my, this is quite the place you have here. So many nooks and crannies to keep secrets. No matter. I have all the time in the world to tear this place apart till I find it.

"And you." Her eyes were back on Nancy. "Keeping low, hiding all these years. Staying out of sight so the rest of us don't know about you. Very sneaky, but now I've found you."

Nancy stammered while taking a couple sidesteps toward Edna. "I don't know what you are talking about. Now, please. Leave!"

"I want the bukvar back. I know you stole it!"

"I don't know what you are talking about."

Anca took another step forward, raising her finger in front of her face to point it at Nancy. "I will tear this place apart to find it. I will tear you apart, if I must."

The tiger loomed behind Anca, filling the doorway. Its frightening gaze never left Nancy's. Despite being large, its features looked stretched, like it was too long and thin. Nancy had never stood next to one of these cats before, but she had a feeling this one was larger than normal.

Those eyes, though. Nancy had seen those eyes. So expressive, so full of emotions. It had to be the same tiger she had seen on the hood of her car only a few days before. But those eyes, those golden-rimmed eyes, held … knowing.

Nancy tried to inch sideways toward her friend.

Anca glared, and the tiger growled as it took a step inside the foyer. Anca raised her hand at Nancy and shot her fingers out from her closed fist. Something hit Nancy square in the chest, throwing her back, knocking the wind out of her. Her head whipped back and cracked into the wall. Plaster sprayed out from the impact, and dust flew from her face.

Anca spewed forth a string of words that sounded like cursing. She glared at her hand held in front of her like it had done something wrong.

To her side, Nancy saw the shape of her friend, holding something long and thin in her hand. Edna sneezed again, unable to contain her allergies. Nancy tried to focus on what was in Edna's hand but the crack against the wall had caused her eyesight to go a bit blurry.

"No, Edna—" The words caught in her throat as the pain from the blow to her head caught up with her. The space around her moved in waves, threatening to topple her. She reached out to the small table against the wall for support. She just needed to stand, make it to her gun, or a phone, but she couldn't see or think. Everything was happening so fast.

Anca shouted angry foreign words Nancy couldn't understand. Edna edged toward Anca with … was that a fireplace poker in her hand? Nancy shook her head. *No, not like this, you need to run!*

She turned to the side to yell at Edna, but words were not able to form in her mouth. Anca raised her hand again, her lips moved ever so slightly and flung her fingers out again.

"Edna!" Nancy finally managed to yell at the top of her lungs. She could hear the panic in her own voice.

Edna's eyes went wide; pain and fear danced on her face. Then she went slack, falling to the floor like a sack of potatoes.

Rage filled Nancy as she watched her friend crumple. She began to reach for the poker.

Suddenly, Anca screamed, a bloodcurdling, painful wail. Nancy turned to see Anca being pulled backwards by an invisible force. Anca struggled to move, to take a step. Her arms flailed wildly as she railed against whatever was pulling her back through the doorway and out onto the sidewalk.

Once she was past the threshold. Anca stopped moving. She stopped screaming and looked around, confused. She touched her middle, a mild look of perplexity and frantic stress on her face.

Despite the pain in her head, Nancy had to chuckle. "But only for a minute," she said to Anca, realizing her limited invitation must have been binding.

Anca looked up at Nancy, her mouth twisted in rage. "You!"

The massive tiger filled Nancy's field of vision, as if to remind her he was still there. Its reeking breath bore down on her. Anca had somehow been pulled out of her house by some unseen force, but her vicious minion was still inside.

Anca seemed to come to this conclusion at the same time and barked an order. The tiger's head snapped up in response, its predatory eyes boring into Nancy's sockets. Nancy tasted blood in her mouth and shivered.

Her mind screamed. She wasn't sure if her mouth made the same sound. Terror overwhelmed her senses, preventing her from hearing anything but an unbridled roar as the tiger's massive blood-stained paw came crashing down on her head.

CHAPTER 17

THE SMELL OF ROTTEN MEAT woke her up and made her stomach roil.

Then the pain overpowered the smell.

Not a sharp pain, but a dull one on the entire right side of her head, telescoping from the back to her jaw. She kept her eyes closed as she breathed in the horrible scent again.

God, what are these people eating in here? She tried to move but found her arms were immobile, bound behind her.

That's when she tried to yell, only to realize that a foul-smelling rag had been crammed into her mouth, allowing only a muffled moan to escape.

Nancy wretched, dry heaving, trying as best she could not to throw up. She worried where the foul bile from her stomach would end up, not having anywhere to go with the rag in her mouth.

She opened her eyes and looked around. The room she was in was at least thirty feet wide in both directions. It reminded her of a warehouse or a partially constructed floor on a skyscraper. Two steels doors led out through two different walls. The floor beneath her was old, worn wood, something not commonly found in a warehouse. Three small windows with arched peaks on top lined the wall opposite her. They were uncovered and dark. Must still be nighttime.

A wave of dull pain spread across her head. She winced and sucked in a breath, which made her stomach churn again, threatening to expel its contents.

Nancy closed her eyes and concentrated on a single dot of light in her vision, an exercise her mother had taught her decades ago to control wild terrors and focus her mind. The pounding of blood in her temples lessened and her frustration and terror abated. Her jaw relaxed, reducing the overwhelming need to wretch and make a bad situation worse.

She looked around more at her prison.

A dark wood podium stood between two desks covered in heaps of papers, books, and candles. The space directly in front of the podium was cleared of the clutter that littered the rest of the room. A six-sided star had been drawn in white chalk with a large black circle surrounding it, just touching the tips of each point. Dusty, unlit red and black candles were spaced around the circle, while an oddly familiar character was scribbled in the middle, similar to the ones she had seen in her house.

The whole macabre setting filled Nancy with dread. She didn't know where she was or where Edna was.

She continued to scan the perimeter of the large room. Three cages littered the outskirts of the space, along with a multitude of boxes next to one of the steel doors. She glanced at the windows again, certain she had seen that style before but not sure where to place them.

The steel door in the wall to her right opened and Nancy caught the dim light showcasing a stout shadow that walked through it.

Anca entered. Nancy suddenly remembered where she had seen those windows. She must be in the rest of the upstairs behind Anca's apartment, probably through the door Anca had yelled at her for touching.

The light from the other room illuminated the cages next to the door, and in one of them was the unmoving shape of Edna Maddox. Trepidation flooded Nancy as she stared at her friend. Edna's chest rose and fell.

Well, that is something.

Just as the door was closing, however, Nancy caught the shadowed shape of another entity in the room. Situated just to the left of Edna's cage was the tiger, sitting calmly on his haunches, watching Nancy. She had missed it before, but now that she knew where to look she could see the reflective eyes of the beast staring at her constantly.

Nancy heard the distinct shuffle of metallic chains as the tiger looked over to its master. As it turned its head, Nancy caught the glimpse of a large manacle around its neck. The thick iron chains, anchored into the concrete wall, were taut as it leaned toward the cage where Edna lay just out of reach.

Anca strode across the room and pulled the rag out. Nancy dry-heaved one more time as her mind lingered on the smell of the rag. She could still smell the foul stench, though, as the rag now hung loosely around her neck. Stale coffee smell from Anca's breath helped Nancy get over the wretched rotten meat aroma.

"Good to see you awake. Is the head still hurting?"

Nancy glared back. She wanted to scream, spit, and kick. She wanted to knock this woman out, but she needed to develop a plan.

"Silent treatment." Anca sauntered over to one of the desks and placed a cup down. Wisps of steam dissipated into the air, causing Nancy's mouth to salivate.

Anca seemed different. She almost seemed cordial, a far cry from how she was acting at Nancy's house. How long had it taken Anca to drag them back here to her lair? What time was it?

Nancy's mind went to dark places, wondering what Anca was going to do to them. She looked back at the tiger and shivered.

"No matter. I only need two bits of information from you. The first is how to get into your library. Seems you have it locked down pretty well in there. It's so nulled that I can't even tell if it exists, but he was able to notice it." Anca waved her hand backward into the darkness toward the tiger.

Nancy stared at the tiger's eyes, unblinking in the darkness. How could a tiger notice a library that a grown woman wasn't able to see, and what was this null business? It was the second time Anca had mentioned that word.

Anca picked up the steaming cup and sipped at the beverage. She breathed in the steam for a moment, relishing the smell before putting down the cup.

"It's good that you're awake. It will make it so much more enjoyable to torture the information out of you, but I will spare you the pain if you simply tell me where it is."

"Where what is?" Nancy tried to remember why she had let Anca into her home, but that seemed ages ago. What was she thinking?

"The bukvar? Grimoire? I need the *Book of Endless Shadow!*" Anca screamed, slamming her hand down on the desk. Dark liquid sloshed out of the cup and spilled on the desk, soaking into some papers.

Nancy remembered what Peter had said about the book in his letter. Maybe it was a book of spells that Anca was using to torture him. She glanced at the podium, noting the lack of a book there. That had to be what Anca was so desperate to find. How did Peter even know to take it? Sudden clarity about Peter and Anca solidified in her head. Anca seemed to have some kind of magical abilities and was using a book of spells that Peter had stolen from her. Anca was also in charge of the tiger.

If Anca, like Ushatgeeta, was a witch, Linda probably was one as well.

A dark pit of despair opened in her mind at realizing just how evil Anca was and hoping she hadn't been unleashing her fury on the poor boy. Nancy thought it had just been emotional abuse, but knowing what she knew now about Anca, she dared not think about what horrible atrocities the kid had been put through.

Anca looked down, her demeanor softening. "Oh, now look what you make me do. That does not bode well for you, now does it?"

Anca twirled her fingers and the spilled coffee seemed to reverse. Like watching a videotape backwards, the dark liquid lifted out of the papers, flew into the air, and deposited itself back into the cup.

Anca picked up the steaming cup again and sipped it. She put it down and grinned.

Nancy looked dumbfounded. "What was that? How did you do that?"

Anca's eyes narrowed as she looked at Nancy. "You aren't very bright, are you? Now how do you manage so many specialized enchantments at your home but not recognize a simple translocation spell?"

Anca took a couple steps forward, squinting in an odd way, like she needed to focus on some feature on Nancy's head, but not on top, behind perhaps?

"Curious. You have the spark. You exude power, that is clear, but …" Her cold eyes went out of focus again, like she was trying to remember where she'd placed her keys.

Anca put her thumb on Nancy's forehead. Icy cold shot into Nancy like a spike. Every instinct told her to jerk back, but she was unable to move. Anca spread out her fingers over the top of her skull, reminiscent of Ushageeta doing the same, but this time it was painfully cold instead of overly warm.

The cold shot down her spine, opposite to Ushageeta's in that it had a thread of heat along with it, just barely taking the edge off the feeling. It wasn't painful, but it was disconcerting, invasive, and far too personal. Every nerve in her body responded in justifiable retribution. Pins and needles danced across every inch of her skin.

Suddenly, the sensation was gone. Anca pulled her hand back.

"Latent, for sure, but I cannot explain why you have such powerful enchantments woven into you and your house. Who nulled your house?"

"I don't know what you're talking about. I don't know anyone who can do … whatever it is that you're talking about."

"You don't? Well, we shall see about that. I suppose I should have just gone right to the pain; it always seems to loosen tongues."

Anca traced Nancy's jawline with a long, icy fingernail, from one ear, across her chin, and back again, leaving cruel, angry lines across her skin. Anca's eyes were intense, with little bolts of electricity sparking around her iris. Nancy's jaw ebbed with energy on the places where Anca had traced.

Anca reared her hand back and slapped Nancy.

Far more severe than a simple slap, the pain seared through Nancy's body, forcing her muscles to contract all at once. Her back arched; her bound wrists pulled at her shoulders. The pain of having her arms wrenched in their sockets, however, was nothing compared to the anguish pounding in her head.

It was like someone had taken white-hot fireplace pokers and was slowly pushing them into her eye-sockets. A stream of jet-fueled fire seemed to envelope her.

She would have screamed, but she couldn't breathe. Her lungs burned. The pain intensified and her vision, already clouded by tears and sweat, began to go dark.

The torture ended abruptly. Like a switch, one second it was there, the next it was gone.

She tried to breathe in, but her lungs spasmed, not allowing any air to stay in them long enough to make it to her bloodstream. Panic set in as the room continued to get darker and darker.

Nancy.

That voice again. She managed to slow her breathing.

Nancy.

Another breath, this time a gulp. She gained a tiny bit of vision back as her head throbbed over and over to the blood pulsing through it. Each pump of her heart caused her brain to cry out in agony.

Nancy.

Something stood in her path, in her vision. Not something, someone, and … did they glow?

Nancy. The familiar voice, the one that had been following her around, was back. *Hold on a little longer, the pain will pass.*

She pulled in a little more oxygen, her lungs slowly releasing their stranglehold on her, slowing their spasms. Her head lolled and she couldn't focus her vision on anything but the shimmering humanoid shape in front of her.

Her lungs finally abating their cries for help; Nancy was able to pull in a nearly full breath. The air stung the insides of her oxygen-deprived lungs, burning them on the way down.

"So what do you think about that, eh?" Anca walked in front of Nancy, or she thought she did. A blob went in front of her vision and blocked the light as it passed.

Nancy couldn't spare the breath to respond, but she did notice a brighter blue shape to the left, like a fuzzy cloud in the corner of her vision. The blob was starting to become sharper, as if someone was slowly turning the lens of a camera before her eyes.

"Don't worry, we're just getting started, aren't we? There is plenty where that came from. Now where is the grimoire?"

Nancy opened her mouth, more because she could barely control her own facial muscles than anything, willing her vision to focus in on the blue cloud.

Anca grabbed her head and yanked to the right. Nancy cried out in pain again. Her muscles were tight and sore, and the sudden forced movement hurt like hell. She felt something pop in her neck.

Anca laughed as she took a step away, out of Nancy's fuzzy vision.

Nancy blinked a couple times, her eyesight clearing. Her eyes stung from the sweat that dripped off her forehead.

The blue cloud floated a few feet in front of her.

Anca walked in front of her, blocking the blue haze in the distance. Nancy managed to sit up a little straighter, and hold her head upright rather than cocked to the side.

"So you ready to talk yet?"

Nancy tried to speak, but her mouth hurt and her tongue seemed like it was too swollen to allow her to form proper sounds.

"Well?" Anca threw her hand forward and something jolted Nancy. It wasn't as painful as last time, but it still hurt like the devil himself had rammed a sword through her leg.

Nancy managed to cry out, her scream trembling in pitch and tone.

Despite the pain, Nancy's vision began to clear. She was finally able to make out the facial features of Anca.

Anca was darker somehow. It was hard to pinpoint exactly what had changed; Nancy supposed it was her vision playing tricks on her.

After what seemed minutes but was probably a few seconds, Anca finally released her hold on Nancy's nerves.

Nancy slumped forward, to the left this time, trying to ease the pain best she could. She huddled over, panting for a bit, trying to catch her breath.

When she finally sat up and opened her eyes, she could see.

CHAPTER 18

I'M SO SORRY, MY DEAR; so very sorry you have to be put through this.

The voice wasn't Anca's. It had a slight Asian accent, old and female. A memory tugged at Nancy's mind. She realized that blue haze was in front of her again, only this time it had a much more defined shape, that of a woman. Short, and round with long braids down her chest.

Nancy gasped in surprise, her mind reeling from the pain still and her shoulder still throbbing. She was hallucinating.

This is what the end is like, isn't it? I'm now going to see my life flash before my eyes. I'm going to relive all my painful memories as Anca slowly tortures my life into oblivion.

Well, you don't have to be so bleak. Dying isn't all that bad, the voice said back to her.

She focused again on the person-shaped blueness in front of her.

Nancy blinked. She couldn't believe her eyes. The pain had been so intense. She had to be dreaming. Was that really Linda sitting on one of the desks? It couldn't be. She was so … incorporeal.

Nancy opened her mouth to try to say something, but her body would not respond. What was wrong with her? Linda was dead, had been for nearly a week.

No, she was hallucinating. It was the pain, mixed with the lack of sleep. Maybe this was what people talked about when they said your life flashed before your eyes when you died. She was starting to go back over her timeline, the things in her life she had accomplished, and relive them one by one.

Nancy Moon was dying. She wouldn't be on this earth anymore. She thought about the Faeries tending to her hurt ankle when she was a child. She wanted to linger on the memory, but the pain in her head snapped her back to reality.

Linda smiled at Nancy, then turned her head to Anca, and frowned.

Oh Anca, how much you have changed, Linda said, her voice distant and small, yet oddly clear in Nancy ears.

Yup, I'm losing my mind.

It really was Linda Hamada. Nancy finally recognized the face, despite it not being all cut up.

"Wha?" Nancy managed to say out loud.

The blue-haze Linda put her finger to her lips and pursed them. *Shh, Anca can't see me, best to keep it that way for now. I can hear your thoughts if you direct them at me though.*

Linda?

Linda smiled. It was warm and inviting and so heartfelt that Nancy began to cry.

"What is happening?" Nancy blurted out, tears pouring down her face. She had meant that as a thought, but it came out as a yell.

At the noise, Anca and turned around from where she was at her desk, bent over, studying something.

"So you can finally talk, can't you? It's about time."

Ignore her, Nancy, look around while you can. You are finally seeing things that you couldn't see before. The pain, it intensifies your abilities. Fight or flight, only this time it's bringing out your magic to help save your life.

Nancy caught the hint of blue again to the right, and, with immense willpower, managed to get her head facing the right direction.

She looked at Edna and the tiger, but she also saw two other ghostly blue forms, seemingly inside of Edna and the tiger.

Edna's spirit, for she had no other word that could describe what she was seeing, was short and round and essentially looked like a ghostly version of Edna.

But the tiger was another matter. Nancy gasped. Instead of the tiger spirit she expected to see, there was a young Asian man.

"Peter."

The words passed her lips so quietly that Anca couldn't have possibly heard them, but the ghost of Linda, standing right next to Nancy now, hunched down and, looking in the same direction, nodded in agreement.

Now you see. Now you see the answer you've been looking for.

Nancy's mind reeled. She opened her mouth to speak, but clamped it down again, not wanting to make noise. Anca had returned her attention to the book on her desk busy reading something with one finger and clutching a couple small pouches in her other hand.

Are they ... dead?

No, but you're seeing past the veil now. Your powers are coming into their own. Pain has that benefit. You are starting to see, dear one. See what you've been missing all your life.

A quote from a movie popped into Nancy's head.

I see dead people?

Linda chuckled at the quote. *I suppose you do, dear, but it's much more than that. You are finally seeing the nature of things. You see better than I ever did when I was alive. You are special; you are magical. You might have seer abilities.*

You mean I see this when I'm being tortured to death? Nancy's strength was beginning to come back into her body, and apparently a snarky attitude came with it.

I wouldn't put it that way, but I suppose it might have a little bit of truth to it. I'm sorry, dear, but just because I'm a witch, or was one when I was still alive, doesn't mean that I know everything. Magic is complicated, and I was actually a very young witch in the grand scheme of things. Anca is far older and wiser than I, and even she wasn't nearly as powerful as some others. Ghost Linda walked around Nancy to the other side of Anca and peered over Anca's arm to see what she was reading.

Nancy glanced over at Edna and the tiger now. She saw the glint of the tiger's eyes peering back, unblinking at her. She shuddered then concentrated on the spirit of the man trapped inside the beast. He was asleep, his eyes darting back and forth erratically. His face had the look of someone in the throes of horror.

Peter's nightmare.

Unfortunately, yes. He started changing soon after he moved here. Probably the presence of magic from Anca and I. Of all the places for him to move, he had to move in next to two witches. Normally his kind has friends and family to help them through the transition, but he didn't. Instead, he found Anca, and she had other interests in mind. She kept his condition hidden from me, so I didn't notice until it was too late.

Nancy tried to make sense of what Linda was saying. *Transition? Changing? Is he a werewolf?*

Linda smiled. *Very astute. A were-tiger, to be specific. They hail mostly from China and India, though where they originally came from is anyone's best guess. I would assume that his family are most likely all were-tigers. The trait is usually hereditary, though not always, but it only shows up in Asian bloodlines.*

Nancy's heart sank at that notion. She remembered the look on his face when he discussed his family. No wonder his father didn't want him to leave.

I have to help him. Nancy pulled against her restraints.

No, you need to get out of here. You must understand. He's under her spell. If you were more progressed with your magic, I might be able to help you, but I don't even know where your affinities lie and what skills you are naturally drawn to. You have impressive latent power, that is for sure. It's the reason I was able to call to you when I lay dying, why I thought you were a witch when I met you. I was partially correct, but I was misled by the power of your potential, and not by your skill. You have no chance against her. I have a plan to get you out of here, but you have to promise me you'll take Edna and run.

It took her a moment to process all the information.

The pieces fit. Peter was the tiger. He was the one that had killed Linda, but he did it by the forceful bidding of Anca. He had been abused, just not in the way Nancy thought.

What do I need to do?

Linda smiled and floated closer. *You need to escape; you need to get your friend over there to safety.*

But how?

Leave that up to me. I know how to get Anca to leave long enough to get you and Edna out of here and to safety. Repeat after me.

Nancy nodded, anticipation building in her stomach.

Nancy repeated everything word for word as it came out of ghost-Linda's mouth. Nancy found it rather easy to do so; she even had a surprising hint of an Asian accent as she spoke.

"I remember when we first met. It was in upstate New York."

Anca looked up, confusion on her face. "What did you say?"

"You thought Woodstock was a coven meeting. You showed up in this long dress, flowers in your hair and an air about you that screamed hippie, but you were obviously in the wrong place at the wrong time. You stood out so much."

Anca huffed, a bewildered look in her eyes. Nancy continued to repeat Linda's words.

"Remember that winter in the Adirondacks? Trapped up in the mountain with nothing but our shawls to keep us warm?"

Anca's eyes grew wider and wider as Nancy kept relaying the message, her bottom lip quivering ever so slightly.

"That was the time you first kissed me, opened my eyes to a whole world of secrets that will most likely remain unspoken for the rest of your life. I was so young, so inexperienced, in both witchcraft and romance. You took my virginity away from me then. We even toyed with summoning a succubus to join in the play, but you hiccuped during the summon and all we ended up with was a sputtering mass of goo that we had to banish back to the other side."

Anca backed up; first one step, then another. She raised her hands to her sweat-covered face. Her eyes shone fright as her stare darted around the room. "Linda?" Her voice was timid and wavering. "Linda, is that really you?"

Nancy replied, "It is, Anca dear. You couldn't leave well enough alone. I wanted out. I wanted a simple life, a life with you. Why did it have to end?"

Anca seemed to get ahold of her emotions and stopped backing up. "You were always so shortsighted, so naive." She continued to glance around, looking at all the corners of the room. "Show yourself!"

"Oh, but I cannot. You sent him to kill me, do you not remember? I cannot take a corporeal form."

"But you can talk through this witch, can't you? I can force you. I can. You see, while you've been playing herbalist, being an utter disgrace to our profession, I've been working on a plan, a plan for greatness. The dreams started a year ago, calling to me. The way has been prepared. The gate will open. All those worthy will gaze upon his face in terror."

Anca stared directly at Nancy at this point, and her gaze bored into her with a discomfort that Nancy had never experienced.

Anca continued. "I had a feeling you had been tagging along, whispering into this bitch's ear the whole time. You took the figurine from me, my link to the beast. I knew you had to have given it to her. I was waiting for her to give it back, but no, you kept it from me. Now where is it? Is it with the book?"

Anca turned to grab something from the desk. It was a hairbrush with a stained wooden handle and natural looking bristles.

Linda stepped into the space between the podium and Nancy, in the middle of the circle to block Nancy from watching Anca. Anca began to chant over the hairbrush while standing in the circle.

Linda spoke through Nancy's mind again. *The figurine was given to Peter by his father when he left home. It was the key to keeping him from turning into what he is now. Anca took it and twisted the magic to bend him to her will while in that form.*

So I should have given it to him the first time I saw him?

Nancy felt regret wash over her. All this, all the deaths and the pain Peter was going through could have been avoided if she had just given the figurine to him. He could have gotten out sooner, and they wouldn't be in this situation right now.

You are not to blame. I stopped you each time. If you had given it back to him before now, she would have been able to continue the spell, but since I took it from her and gave it to you, her bond with him is weaker than it's ever been. I know I told you to return it, but you did well in keeping it from Anca. Once I died, I was able to see clearly, to fully understand the nature of the figurine, and I realized I had given you erroneous information. I bound myself to you through your act of kindness and selflessness to stay here in this world, to follow you around, to help keep you from making the same mistake I made.

But what if I had given it to him? Would he have been able to take control?

No. Linda's ghost seemed to sigh. *He would have come back here and Anca would have simply taken it from him.*

"Where are you, you whore?" Anca interjected. She followed Nancy's gaze to the center of the circle and grinned. She mumbled some kind of incantation and flung her fingers in the direction of Linda.

It could have been her eyes playing games, but Nancy could swear that the image of Linda was less translucent now. Almost like she could reach out and touch her, assuming she didn't have her hands still bound.

"I can see you now." She pointed the hairbrush at Linda and with a loud, clear voice spoke, "I bind your immortal soul to the sigil on which you stand and key you to the brush that one graced your head." Sparks fizzled between the brush and Linda.

Nancy blinked. "What happened," she asked.

Anca gave her a glare but immediately looked back at Linda.

She tried to bind me to the brush, but failed. I knew she has been planning something for a while now, so most of my items of power have been spelled to counteract anything she tried to use on me. I've known she was up to no good, but I didn't know the depths of it if she's preparing to find the Gate. This is much worse than I thought. Her ghostly visage displayed a worried expression

Before Nancy had the chance to ask what Linda meant about the gate, Anca hissed and spat at the ghost. "You bitch! At least you are bound to the circle. I will return with something you haven't spelled."

With that, Anca whirled around and marched for the steel door leading back to her apartment.

CHAPTER 19

ANCA STORMED OUT OF THE room, slamming the metal door behind her. The sound hurt Nancy's ears as it echoed through the cavernous warehouse. She glanced at Edna, who still remained unconscious in the cage, and shivered at the sight of the tiger next to the doorway. She needed to get to Edna, but the tiger, no, Peter, was in the way.

Was he really the same beast that had jumped on top of her car? The same one that had killed Linda? The whole ordeal was so surreal that Nancy didn't have time to process it. She just needed to react.

Something akin to cool water touched her skin. It was the incorporeal form of Linda. She jumped at the odd touch then shook with fright as her skin crawled.

She's going to go find something of mine in order to bind me, but she'll have to test each thing with a spell to find out if I trapped it or not. You only have a few minutes, so please hurry.

"How can you … are you real?"

Linda smiled. *Of course I am, dear. As real as you. And you are special in that you can see me.* Linda's ghostly eyes that lacked any color seemed to fade in and out. Nancy got the feeling she was reliving something from her past.

You have grown quite a bit since my death. I am sorry you had to be there to see me die.

"I'm sorry you had to die."

Linda gave a wistful smile, but then pursed her lips and gained a serious expression. *Now quick, can you get yourself out of the ropes?*

Nancy remembered that she had the solution on her wrist. *Thank you, Edna.* "I have a bracelet that conceals a small knife in it. If you can undo the clasp, I might be able to get it opened and cut the ropes."

Linda smiled. *Not a problem. I can help.*

Linda floated toward Nancy, the passed through her. A deep chill penetrated her body as it happened, causing her to shudder once again.

Oh, I'm so sorry. I keep forgetting that you can feel that, Linda said.

"No problem. I am still not used to this whole thing of being a witch. Is there a school?"

Ghost Linda laughed, an echo-filled hollow sound that made Nancy squirm. There is no school, but you do need to be taught.

Nancy scrunched up her face.

You are a witch, and a fairly powerful one from what I can sense. Nancy felt penetrating cold around her wrists as Linda tried to undo the clasp that was out of Nancy's reach. *It's curious why you didn't start becoming one until this late in life. It usually shows up at puberty. Was your mother a witch?*

Nancy was taken aback. "No, my parents are just regular people, at least I think they aren't magical. Both in their eighties. They live in Maine."

Linda, still behind her, grunted. There was a click, and the bracelet that Edna had given her what seemed so long ago, unbuckled and slid down her wrist to her open hand.

"Thank you." She found the button and pushed. A small blade popped out of the bracelet, allowing her to saw through the ropes.

Linda appeared back in her vision. *Very smart of her, by the way.*

"Who?"

Edna. That girl sure knows her stuff.

"She does." Nancy was partway through the rope and could feel it loosen.

With a tug and some serious pain, Nancy pulled. The rope came apart and she finally managed to get her hands together in front of her. She quickly undid herself the rest of way, severing the bonds at her feet, and pulling off the remaining loops around her wrists. She rubbed them for a second as she ran over to see Edna.

Before she got there, she froze. The tiger was looking at her; its breathing had quickened. It licked its chops and arched its back, straining against the chain holding it to the wall.

"Easy, kitty." Visions of the damage this exact cat had done flashed in her mind.

She is a good friend for you, to be taking this kind of abuse in your name.

"I know," Nancy replied. She felt a stab of regret for getting Edna into this. How had things escalated so quickly since finding a dying woman in an alleyway only a week ago? She inched forward, hoping the chains holding the beast at bay were strong enough. Sweat glistened on her palms, and a lingering hint of vomit hit her nostrils. She felt weak in the knees, but she ignored the threat and focused on what the next step was.

She finally got to Edna's cage without the cat moving and let her eyes travel from the killer to the lock that kept her friend confined.

Dammit! It was locked.

Check Anca's desk. She was never one for keeping things in pockets or wearing them on herself, Linda replied, her ghostly visage calling to her from the circle still.

Nancy turned, seeing the tiger again. It lay on its front paws, eyes watching her. Big, sad eyes. "I'm so sorry you are mixed up in this."

Nancy's dream from the night before flooded her mind. She remembered the plea of the Chinese woman.

Peter's mother.

Nancy ran back to Anca's desk, and sure enough the keys were lying on the top corner, under a pile of yellowed papers containing characters similar to the ones she'd been seeing recently. She wondered if this was the language of the witches, something she would have to learn in order to cast spells.

While you're there, open the top drawer to the other desk. Nancy gave Linda a curious glance but complied. *Under the lip will be a small metal switch, pull it.*

Nancy did and a small door on the side of the desk popped open. *There should be some papers in there. They are the deed to my herb shop. I want you to have it. Better you than Anca.* As promised, a sealed envelope was the only thing in the tiny drawer. She pocketed the papers and slammed the small hidden door and drawer closed.

To think I'm so close to where I lived the last year. Her voice, already distant and frail, grew more so. Nancy supposed it was, given that she was hearing it with her own ears. The thought gave Nancy pause.

I'm talking to a ghost, she finally admitted to herself.

Linda chuckled, her ghostly voice echoy and haunting in it's pitch. *You are that, my dear. You are that.*

Nancy kneeled down in front of the cage. "I keep thinking that I am dreaming. Like this is just stress-induced paranoia. The adrenaline is keeping me on my feet, but I worry that eventually I'm going to wake up or come to in a hospital bed with tubes down my throat and a bevy of nurses rushing around me."

Linda's reply took on a serious tone. *No, you are not dreaming, I'm afraid. I realize this isn't something that you are normally taught in kindergarten, but a lot of the fairy tales are true. The world is a much bigger place than you can imagine.*

"How so?"

Nancy unlocked the cage door and began to shake Edna, who moaned. Nancy was glad she was alive. She blinked to stave off tears of joy when she heard the sound.

Linda chuckled. *How I wish I was still alive. I would have loved to take you under my wing. But alas, there is no time. I'm not long for this world. Soon Anca will return and bind me, possibly use me and you for her will. That is why it's so important that you get out of here, my dear. I can't have you remaining when she gets back.*

"But what about you?" Nancy worked on pulling her friend out.

Linda sighed. *I'm afraid I'm somewhat tied to this fellow here.* She pointed to the tiger, the one still looking at Nancy with those big, sad eyes. *Since she controls him, she controls me.*

A tear finally escaped Nancy's eye and rolled down her cheek. "Is there anything I can do to help you?"

No, dear, you have done all that you can do. Now get Edna and run. Get back to your house; it's the safest place in the city.

Nancy looked at the chained tiger to the side of her. Its piercing gaze locked back. Her heart fell as she saw not only his tiger form, but also the boy's spirit inside of him.

"I promised to help him and I failed. It's all my fault that he is here right now."

No, you need to get out of here. We've spent too much time as it is. You must go! There is a fire escape to the other alley on the opposite wall. The door sticks a bit, but it opens to the outside where you can get down the fire ladder.

"I can't leave you to be a slave to Anca." Beside her. Edna began to sit up, holding her head.

She looked down at the keys still in her hand and up at the tiger—no, Peter—then turned to Linda. "I am sorry for all the pain you have had in your life; I wish we could have been friends earlier to have some better memories."

CHAPTER 20

A NCA PETRAN WAS IN A panic. She'd been all over their bedroom searching for items of power that Linda used to use. Even as a ghost, Linda was powerful and had apparently recognized Anca's ulterior motives for moving to Madison. She finally found a bottle of wine in the cellar that she knew Linda had not taken the time to spell.

Her preparation for capturing Nancy would have to wait. She could probably throw her into one of the cages. Having Linda here, now? Anca could use the same spell on Linda first, and then she would need more reagents to cast it a second time.

It took five steps into the room before Anca realized something was off in her warehouse.

"Took you long enough," Nancy stated with an air of superiority, like she wasn't the one tied up and about to be tortured. Anca would enjoy teaching this woman some manners before she enslaved her to do her bidding.

She scrutinized the cages to her left, spying Nancy's petulant human friend, still unconscious and right where Anca had left her behind bars. She nodded at the theran, still chained up. The tiger blinked at her before putting his hungry eyes back on the woman in the chair.

You will have your fill when I am done.

The friend wasn't magical at all and would be useless for the spell she had prepared.

Still, tension ticked in her mind that something in here had changed, and it was probably Linda's fault.

Damnable woman. You will be mine soon.

She looked back at her torture victim, sitting on the chair in the middle of the room, in line with both her and Linda's old desks.

The barely visible outline of Linda remained trapped in the prepared circle. The temporary binding spell would only last for so long, but this bottle of wine would be enough to keep her there permanently, or at least long enough for her to transfer her spirit to something more powerful.

Being able to draw upon the magic of a captured spirit could be a powerful thing. If all went will she could eventually conscript her spirit into that of a djinni. It would be a long, arduous spell, but once she had the book back, she would be able to perform the ritual.

He would be pleased.

Linda had the audacity to walk back into her life and offer up her spirit for use. It wasn't what she had planned. It was better.

Her army was beginning to come together. She had the beast, who she could keep forced in tiger form whenever she needed, outside of the moon cycle. Her bond to him was beginning to weaken, but she would have the grimoire back soon and would be able to renew the connection before the full moon.

She had Linda's spirit from which she could draw power. Linda had always been a powerful mage but hadn't used that power properly. She would tap into it from time to time, but she never seemed to fully embrace the reality of her life as a witch.

And now she had Nancy Moon. A new witch who had somehow not transitioned at puberty, but instead had done so later in her life. All that untapped power would be something anyone would kill for.

All the better for Anca. She could train her properly. Use her for whatever she needed. If she didn't get Nancy's cooperation, that was fine. If not, she could take what she needed by force.

But first she needed the book. Dragon would want it back for sure. She was surprised he hadn't set his two trolls against her. It was just a matter of time before they would come knocking, but by the time they showed up, demanding the grimoire back, she would be long gone, living in Nancy's house with some of the most sophisticated nullicants she had ever felt woven into the very fabric of the walls, floor, roof, and grounds.

Oh, she would enjoy pulling that house apart bit by bit until she unraveled its mysteries.

Anca stopped in front of her desk, sifting through the various reagents she would need for the permanent binding spell, lost in thought.

"Well? Cat got your tongue?" Nancy laughed like a maniac at her own stupid joke.

Anca grimaced. She needed to shut this woman up so she could focus on securing Linda's spirit. She could torture Nancy all she wanted later, but now she needed uninterrupted focus.

She dwelled briefly on the notion that for the past fifty years she would have normally asked Linda's help in doing the more complicated castings, but now she was turning the tide on her old partner, her old lover.

Linda hadn't seen the vision; she hadn't been called to open the gate. Anca was now serving a higher power.

Her mind bent over itself as she veered to a dark place inside of her, one that had been growing more and more lately. She hadn't spent most of her life touching this type of magic, but it was always there, always useful, and it was incredibly powerful.

Pain!

She screamed as she thrust the power from her fingertips.

Nancy yelped for a brief second before going silent. The spell would spasm her lungs, forcing all air out of her chest to the point she couldn't vocalize anymore. Nancy's back arched and Anca smirked.

That should keep her silent for a bit.

She turned back to her desk and started drawing a binding rune on a silver hand mirror with black lipstick.

Without the ropes binding her wrists together, Nancy had interlocked her fingers behind her back and struggled keeping them together for the duration of the attack spell.

She couldn't concentrate enough to keep her arms behind her. She vaguely remembered grabbing her neck in anticipation of losing the ability to breathe. When she was able to gain control of her faculties again, not having her arms pulled from their sockets made the experience a lot less traumatic.

The pain finally subsided from Anca's latest attack.

Nancy glanced from Edna's form to Peter's then back over to Linda, who was still standing in the circle watching Nancy with a worried look.

Linda spoke once Nancy had regained control of her breathing. *Why did you stay?*

You said she will enslave you. I can't let that happen. The words came slowly, painfully as Nancy tried to form coherent thoughts through her clouded mind.

Linda looked up at her, sadness in her eyes. *Oh sweetheart. Dear Nancy. I just wanted you to escape with Edna over there. You shouldn't have worried about me. My fate is already sealed.*

But you said the capture spell would only last a few minutes. Nancy glanced over to Edna, who was awake but pretending to be asleep. *If we can just buy you more time, then you can escape with us.*

Linda looked at Nancy with a melancholy expression. *You are a dear, but none of us are making it out of this place now. You should have taken your chance.*

Then we should stop worrying about the problem and start working toward a solution.

Pain still clouding her body and ability to think, Nancy spoke to Anca, trying to distract her from her spell casting. "Linda knew you were going to kill her that night."

Anca glanced up at her for a moment, her eyes lacking the recognition that she was actually paying attention. Whatever Anca was concentrating on seemed to be important and easily susceptible to distraction. Nancy was all too happy to help. She couldn't let Linda sacrifice herself. She would grasp onto any hope she could.

Her leg twitched again, a brief shot of pain ran down it. She glanced at Edna and the tiger, hoping she hadn't just made the worst decision of their lives.

"Too scared to do your own dirty work? You probably wouldn't have beat her in a fair fight. Is that why you used Peter over there for all your bidding, killing all those other witches? Because you were too scared of doing the work yourself? Had to get a boy to do it?"

Nancy spit on the ground, spittle mixed with mucus and blood.

"I mean, just look at me. I don't know any magic, but you have to tie me up all the same, don't you? Because you are too scared to even face me one on one. Miss Big Powerful Witch can't handle a little old lady that doesn't have any powers. Is that it?"

Anca spun around, anger flashing in her eyes. "Silence!" She turned back to the circle and started to mutter some inaudible words, holding a jar of mashed herbs in one hand, a paintbrush in another.

Nancy smiled. It was working. "Or you will what? Torture me again? Each time you do it, you're using up the precious energy that you need to do whatever you're doing right now. Let me guess, you're trying to capture Linda? You know she's not even in the circle? She's hanging out over with Peter right now."

Anca paused, glancing quickly over to the cages then back to Linda.

"I said shut up." Her voice was low and tense.

"Or what? Go ahead, hit me again with your powerful whatever that was. I can take it all day long."

Anca pointed to the cages. Her voice was calm and level but her eyes gave away the boiling rage just under the surface. "Or I will hurt your friend over there. How will she be able to take it, huh? You may be able to handle it, due to your innate magic, but what about her?"

Nancy paused. She couldn't have Anca doing that, but she still had to keep Anca distracted. *Forgive me, Edna. I'm really trying to keep her from focusing on you.*

Nancy turned and looked at the tiger. All anger drained out of her voice as she spoke to him from across the room. "You see how she is, Peter? You don't have to live this life anymore. I know what she's done to you and I will do everything I can to prevent it from happening again. You're a wonderful young man with a bright future ahead of you. You don't have to put up with this woman's crazy any longer."

The physical tiger still glared hungrily at her, but the spirit wasn't lying down anymore. His head was up and his eyes focused on her, listening.

Good.

Nancy, what are you doing? It was Linda.

Nancy turned to her new friend and smiled. *I'm getting you some more time. Keep testing the circle and let me know once you can get out.*

"Peter, do you want to see your family again? Do you want to take control of this beast that Anca's brought out in you? I can help you. You don't have to have such nightmares any longer. There is a better way."

Nancy watched the blue-gray spirit as it shifted uncomfortably inside its iron-secured body. The sound of the chains flexing and relaxing was music to her ears.

"Peter, you are young. You have your entire life ahead of you. You have the power within yourself to resist what this woman is doing to you. I believe in you. I have the figurine that Anca used to control your tiger form. I have the book you stole from her to give to me. You already know what she's doing, and you knew how to make it stop. Together, we can fix you."

Anca whirled around, rage boiling in her eyes. "I said shut up! You know I don't need you alive, right? I can do the same thing I'm doing to Linda, harness that power any way I need. I already know the book is in your house. It's just a matter of time before I find it."

Anca's fingers trembled as she breathed in heaping gulps of air. She seemed much larger than usual, and her visage far darker. Her eyes were dull, nothing reflecting in them anymore, which frightened Nancy more than anything else. Strangest of all, there was no hint of the blue-gray spirit that all the others in the room shared. Anca's was mostly gray and black at this point. Little wisps of black smoke curled off her skin, evaporating into the air.

No, I have to keep going, keep her distracted.

Nancy decided to take a leap at what was going on between the different colors of the spirits.

"So you're delving into the dark arts? Little bit of black magic to cap off your day? I can see it pouring off your skin right now. Black wisps. Your eyes are sunken in, and you look worse than you normally do. Now I know why people always called witches crones. You are the epitome of crone-like behavior. Will your skin keep getting more and more wrinkled as you keep going with this? Is there even any turning back?"

The blackness surrounding Anca appeared to find new energy in addition to the wisps of smoke. Little sparks danced across her skin like tiny lightning bolts. They crackled and popped with electrical fury. They were fascinating to behold, but given the circumstances, Nancy wondered if she had pushed Anca too far.

"You bitch! You know nothing about what I have been through! You don't know me and I have had enough of your incessant talking. You are nothing and will always be nothing!"

Anca raised her hands. The black smoke and lighting poured off them in sheets. Sparks danced between her fingers like a Jacob's ladder, beginning at the webbing between her fingers and continuing out to the tips, where they burst in tiny explosions of grimy electricity.

Oh shit. What have I done?

Anca murmured something under her breath and thrust her fingers forward.

Just as she did, the haze around the circle blinked like a lightbulb about to short circuit.

CHAPTER 21

LINDA'S SPIRIT SCREAMED AND JUMPED forward to intercept the wave of sparking blackness that Anca hurled toward Nancy.

Linda took the spell square in the chest. Like water from a fire hose through tissue paper, it tore through her translucent body. Nancy watched in horror as the blackness enveloped and disintegrated the bright blue spirit of Linda Hamada.

For the second time in a week, Nancy watched Linda die.

"No!" Nancy cried as she swung her arms around from behind her and jumped forward, trying to reach the disappearing wisps of blue. She wanted to grab her, pull her out of harm's way, keep her around for a bit longer, but her hands grasped nothing but air.

Instead of hitting her square in the chest, the vastly diminished black blast of energy hit Nancy's left shoulder, spinning her around and toppling her to the floor in a heap. Her left arm spasmed and burned with a solar intensity.

Edna screamed, a mournful wail of anguish.

Anca turned to face the cages, where Edna's scream had distracted her. Edna huddled in the center of the cage, trying to keep her arms and feet away from the paws of the tiger whose chain was just long enough for it to get a meaty paw between the bars. The tiger snarled and pulled on its chain, trying to get at the terrified woman.

"Beast, attack!" Anca threw her hands into the air and the shackle around the beast's neck unhinged and fell away. It lunged at Edna, who cringed further into the back of the cage. The massive paw barely missed tearing her flesh.

"Kill Nancy, you idiot!" Anca screamed. She was limping, hobbling. Her face an amalgamation of rage and pain. She had paid a price for that killing spell.

The tiger turned. A deep-seated urgency for survival welled up in Nancy as the large cat's hungry eyes locked with hers. Her heart pounded in her chest and the taste of blood and the smell of burned hair filled her with fear. Her shoulder burned in agony, and she was forced to scramble backward along the cold floor using one arm. She edged backwards, trying to put some distance between herself and the tiger.

If Nancy and Edna had just ran, they would be safe.

Tears streamed down Nancy's face.

The Tiger-Peter took a few steps forward, stretched his cramped legs, and roared, his venomous eyes bouncing back and forth between Nancy and Anca.

Nancy Moon had killed Linda. It was all her fault.

Anca commanded loud and fast, "Kill HER!" pointing at Nancy.

The tiger took another step forward. It opened its mouth and licked its chops.

Nancy's mind flashed with the notion that this was not just some beast, but this was Peter Lin, whose mother had died when he was young. The same young man that had helped her move boxes downstairs only a few days ago. The man she'd promised Linda she would help then abandoned to Anca's twisted desires.

Nancy had failed him, dooming him to a life of forced servitude.

"Please, Peter," Nancy begged. She backed up against the warehouse wall. The cold brick did not keep her from sweating, but gave her chills in addition to the fear crawling under her skin. "Peter, I'm so sorry. Please listen to me."

Apprehension grew in Nancy. She glanced to the side, at Edna, still inside her cage. The two locked eyes for a brief moment, exchanging a glance that conveyed mutual admiration, respect, and terror. Nancy mouthed the words, "I'm so sorry."

Edna wiped a tear from her cheek and nodded.

That woman.

"Run, Edna, make it out while you can," she said, soft and quiet, inaudible to anyone but her.

A sudden clarity hit Nancy's mind. She knew she was going to die; she knew that now. Only, she would not die lying on her back, cowering. She would face her attacker head on.

"You killed her, you know." Nancy's eyes didn't leave the beast that was slowly padding its way down to her. She spoke in almost a monotone voice, just barely audible for Anca to hear. She didn't know if the tiger could understand, but at this point she didn't care. "That death spell or whatever you were about to do to me, you hit Linda with it."

Anca spun around at the place where Linda had been, then back to Nancy, a wild expression on her face. Shock? Anger? Surprise? Nancy didn't really care.

Despite the wild look in her eyes, Anca appeared physically drained. The blackness that once filled her visage had faded. Like ink dropped into a pond eventually fades into nothingness, whatever power she had surrounded herself with was gone.

Anca's body movements mirrored her drained power. She leaned up against the desk, holding herself up with one hand. Her breaths labored as her chest heaved. She wore a pained and confused expression.

Nancy twisted her body to allow her good arm to start pushing her up from the floor. With some effort, she managed to get herself to a kneeling position. "I will not die lying on my back. I won't give you the satisfaction," Nancy said to Anca.

Anca sneered. "I don't care how you die, but I do hope he takes his time."

Nancy stared into the tiger's eyes. He was nearly to her, slowly padding his way to her doom. She gave him a small smile, which made him pause in his steps.

"I don't know that you will have that satisfaction." Her eyes softened as she looked his his mournful eyes."

"He knew." Nancy whispered.

Anca's expression of derision flashed with concern. "What?"

"Peter knew what you were doing to him. I bet you thought you were so clever, harnessing his power to use for your own ends, but you didn't realize just how strong he was. He knew and he planned. He outsmarted you.

"He knows you don't care for him. Even in this form he's listening, paying attention." Her eyes had not left those large, round, golden eyes of his. She wanted him to see her eyes, see the lack of fear in them. She hoped it was enough to get through to the man underneath the fur and claws.

Anca spat, "He does no such thing. He's just a dumb animal, and I control him."

"Maybe you do control his actions, but you do not control his thoughts. His thoughts are his own. His heart is large and full of love. You can't compete against that. He has so many people that love and care for him, and he knows it. You are playing with things you know nothing about, and you will get burned. You may be able to coerce him for now, but soon you will lose your power over him."

Nancy was calm. Far calmer than she had any right to be. She flashed a bloodstained grin at Anca. "You will never have his love."

"What is taking you so long, you stupid theran?" Anca shrieked, pointing at Nancy again. "Kill the witch!"

Peter slowly loomed over Nancy. The smell of raw meat and overgrown cat breath hit her.

It should have been disgusting, but it only calmed her more.

She looked up at Peter, who turned his head down at her. "You are so strong." Her words were slow, full of caring and decency. She moved to cup his orange face but stopped as her fingertips brushed his fur. "I'm so sorry for failing you, my son. It's not your fault. I should have listened to Linda earlier; I should have trusted my gut."

The tiger didn't move. Could he understand her? Nancy's heart seemed to skip a beat at the thought. She rested her hand on his snout.

the warmth from his breath was terrifying and her hand shook. She had to touch him, let him know he was loved and cared for.

"You didn't kill her, Peter. The burden of guilt is not yours. She gave herself so you could live. She sought me out so you would know she forgives you. And I failed her. She gave me a simple task to save a young man from a terrible predicament, and I failed. I can't ask you to forgive me. I don't deserve that. I only ask that you find peace with yourself. I'm sorry it had to end like this."

She dropped her hand to her side, frowning, fighting back tears that yearned to flow down her face. Shame caused her to look away. "I met your mother. She came to me in a dream. She was so beautiful, so caring. I wish you had gotten to know her."

Nancy lifted her head back up to look into those wide golden eyes. They were darker now. She wondered how much he could truly understand her. "You no longer need to be haunted by those nightmares. You aren't the one doing this, Anca is. I'm sorry you are suffering."

Peter bent down, and opened his mouth. The foul-smelling breath made Nancy want to cringe but she held her ground, waiting for the bite. She closed her eyes from the moisture. A slimy mass of cat tongue scraped across her face as he tasted his victim. Steamy air from his nostrils coated her face as he exhaled.

This was it, her time had come. She braced for the bite.

But none came. Instead, she heard him chuff through his partially open mouth. Short bursts of air exhaled through his lungs almost sounded like a laugh.

What was happening?

Suddenly his presence was gone, as wind caught Nancy's matted hair and swept it up and over her head. She heard a thud and a predatory growl followed by the soft patter of cat paws hitting the wood floor a few feet away.

She opened her eyes hesitantly, scared at what she would see.

The imposing shape of the tiger was no longer hovering above her. Instead, flashes of orange and black fur danced at the periphery of her vision. She turned to get a better look.

Peter padded toward Anca, who backed away from him around the corner of her desk. Blood welled on Anca's shoulder, through her slashed open shirt. Anca's eyes were wide with fright and confusion.

"No, no, no! Back!" Anca thrust out her hands over and over. Little trails of smoke sloughed off her fingers, but nothing else happened other than a couple minor sparks.

"You beast! Heel! I created you!" Anca tripped over a pile of books and stumbled backward, catching herself on the desk.

Anca thrust out a hand again and a stream of sparks tore through the air, catching onto the tiger's coat and sizzling. She murmured something in a foreign language while twirling her fingers. Indigo light sprayed from her hands in violent arcs. Her wild head of hair stood up, flailing as she moved.

Anca turned her body to the side, planted her foot, grounding herself, and bent her knees. She pulled both of her cupped hands backward. Between them she held a pulsing white ball of lightning.

She yelled and thrust her arms out. A flash of yellow and orange filled Nancy's field of view as Peter dodged to the side and zigged back at Anca. He was nearly as fast at the lightning itself.

He slammed into Anca from the side, causing her to release the lightning orb at an angle that arced toward the roof.

A loud explosion boomed as the lightning hit. Fiery wood debris rained down on Nancy as she scuttled to the side to get out of the way. Sparks scattered everywhere, catching parts of the floor on fire.

"Nancy!" Edna yelled, "Over here, let's go!" She had gotten out of the cage that Nancy had left unlocked.

Nancy couldn't turn away from the fight. Fear clenched her throat and her muscles. She barely noticed the pain in her left arm. Anca threw a fireball with one hand, hitting him in the side. The tiger yelped in agony at his burned flesh but swiped at the witch, tearing into her arm and shredding further the loose shirt she wore.

Anca screamed as Peter swiped with his other paw, tearing into her face. She thrust her hands out and lightning poured from her good arm into his chest in cobalt arcs that lit up the inside of the warehouse. He cried out, an agonized, mournful howl of a large jungle cat in pain.

He fell back, stumbling sideways before falling down. Bright red from his gaping wound glistened in the firelight, leaving Nancy feeling raw. It was tearing her up inside that she couldn't seem to move. She couldn't say or do anything to help. She focused on a pinpoint, willing herself out of the shock she was in.

"Peter! Leave her!" Nancy yelled, finally gaining control of her vocal cords.

The tiger glanced at her, his eyes flashing wild with rage and anger. His nostrils flared, steam poured out in a puff, but he turned his attention back to the threat.

Edna locked arms with Nancy. "We need to get out of here. The place is going to burn down!"

Nancy broke her gaze from the two and looked at Edna while red flames danced in her eyes. "We have to help them!" She was hysterical, unable to move, rooted by some unseen force. She felt like a child, crying for no reason other than being overwhelmed by the stress of the situation.

"Anca is too powerful. We can't help him, Nancy. We have to go!" Edna urged.

The wooden rafters of the warehouse were engulfed in flames from Anca's missed spell casting. Edna pulled on Nancy's arm, trying to get her to her feet. Timbers above them began to crack.

"Peter! Leave her, save yourself!" Nancy yelled. She was somehow on her feet, though she didn't realize how she had made it there.

Edna continued to pull on her arm, urging her to exit.

The tiger ignored her, pulling himself back up onto his feet. One of his legs hung limp, possibly broken. Nancy's heart sunk as she noticed the massive gash on his side, ribs exposed, flesh torn and blood on the ground. Anca managed to throw something more at the large cat, sending it flying and landing in a heap. He did not get up but lay twitching on the ground, howling in pain.

"Nancy!" Edna yelled, too close to her ear, snapping her out of her state. "We *have* to go now!"

Edna began dragging her across the floor. Burning timbers fell to the ground all around, one nearly hitting Anca, who managed to deflect it with a spell and fling it at the tiger. His reflexes too slow to move out of the way. Anca flung another spell at the beast, hitting him in his haunches.

He spun around, landing on the floor, his body twitching. His eyes were glazed over and his chest no longer rose and fell. Anca unleashed a last attack at his lifeless body, not seeing the burning timber headed right for her head.

Nancy sobbed but allowed herself to be led out of the warehouse, into Anca's apartment, out onto the metal landing, and down the stairs into the alleyway.

The building above roared with flames. Rivulets of heat bathed off its brick walls, and the entire roof danced with crackling wood. Smoke filled her eyes as she continued to be led out of the carnage like in a dream. She wished it were a dream. She'd utterly failed in all that she was hoping to accomplish.

CHAPTER 22

TEARS CONTINUED TO FLOW DOWN Nancy's cheeks as Edna pulled on her arm, urging her to keep moving. They left the alleyway and made their way onto the street, into a crowd of people.

Sirens wailed in the distance. Nancy barely heard them.

The whole thing was out of her control. Anca had killed him. Peter was dead and it was Nancy's fault. She should have listened, should have run. At least Peter would still be alive.

"Nancy, we need to go," Edna pleaded.

Nancy sighed, scanning over the growing crowd of onlookers.

Two bright blonde heads of hair, a foot higher than the rest, caught her eye, jolting her back to reality.

The two hulking bruisers she and Edna had met in the car a few nights ago were here. While one of them stared intently at the alleyway, the other, the one who had shown his strength by pushing down Edna's car with his fists, scanned the crowd, searching. His eyes were intense as he scrutinized each person.

Realization flooded Nancy, remembering something Anca had said. They were there looking for her, or at least for Anca. They wanted the book back. Who had Anca said they were? Dragon and his henchmen?

Whoever they were, they made Anca nervous. Anyone that caused that sort of reaction in a witch of her status and power wasn't someone to mess with. If they saw Nancy, it wouldn't end well.

"We have to go."

Edna sighed. "That's what I've—"

Nancy crouched down. Her shoulder screamed in pain as her arm twisted in its socket. Her vision went white for a moment before coming into focus again. She willed herself back to reality, nearly fainting from the anguish.

They pushed through the crowd to the back of the street where they were met by a ratty looking hatchback and a young Indian woman with folded arms. Ushageeta's assistant opened up the passenger's door and urged them inside.

Nancy didn't hesitate. She climbed into the backseat, trying to ignore the pain shooting through her shoulder.

The young girl climbed into the drivers' seat and, before Edna had a chance to even get her door fully closed, started the car and took off down the street.

The young woman sped around corners, ignored stop signs, and blew through red lights.

After they were a safe distance away, she slowed the car and spoke.

"Guru sent me to find you. She had a feeling you might need help."

Edna, despite the rough time in the cage, was upbeat. "See, Nan? I told you she was amazing."

Nancy's mind was a whirlwind of emotion. Peter was dead. Anca was still in the burning building when they left. Someone named Dragon and his seven-foot-tall linebacker henchmen were after her. Linda was dead after saving her sorry life. She couldn't think of that now. She couldn't allow the despair that would come with dwelling on past mistakes. There would be time enough later. "I … we appreciate her and your help."

The young girl nodded and continued to drive on.

The city was a blur of buildings as the young woman drove back to the familiar Highlands.

Nancy tried to relax. The searing pain in her shoulder seemed to be abating, allowing her to think. Adrenaline coursing through her veins slowly receded, allowing her mind to wander. She wallowed in her thoughts for the remainder of the trip.

Outside of Nancy's house, Ushageeta was waiting in her wheelchair.

Edna said apologetically. "I may have given her your address."

Nancy grunted and winced as she got out of the car. Getting in wasn't too bad, mostly because of the adrenaline-filled haze she had been in when she had left Anca's building. But sitting in the relatively calm and quiet car for a while had allowed her hackles to lower and the pain in her left shoulder to worsen. She cried out.

"You okay there?" Edna grabbed Nancy's other arm and helped take some of the weight off.

"Yeah, it's just been a rough day. I need sleep." Nancy looked somberly at the house.

Ushageeta's face was heavy with concern. She and Nancy exchanged a look for a few moments before Edna motioned them inside.

Edna smiled. "Come on inside."

Ushageeta didn't move and Nancy wasn't about to let someone in a wheelchair go after her.

Nancy spoke up. "Isn't the door unlocked?"

Ushageeta paused before she said anything. "Well, yes, but … it's *impolite* to just enter someone's house uninvited."

Nancy's remembered Anca being sucked out of her house.

"But only for a minute," Nancy mumbled under her breath.

"What's that?" Edna asked.

Nancy glanced at Ushageeta, realization dawning on her face as she understood that she had the power to keep people from her home. She didn't understand that power, but she had it, somehow. Ushageeta gave a single nod.

"Please come in. You are both welcome in my home as long as you wish." She wasn't sure if the last bit was required, but added it anyway.

Despite Nancy's desire to go to bed and wallow in self-pity, Ushageeta insisted she lie down on the downstairs guest bed where the guru began to fuss over Nancy's injuries.

"What the hell happened?" she barked as she opened up her satchel and rooted around for some herbs.

Nancy was at a loss for words. Her brain continued to grind, but she couldn't form a thought long enough to divert her from the final picture in her mind of Peter's dead tiger body lying motionless in front of Anca.

It was all her fault. She had messed things up. She tried to keep out the despair, but it seeped in around every thought.

Ushageeta found all the herbs she needed and handed them to her assistant to make some tea and a salve.

Edna began talking, telling Ushageeta everything that had happened to the two women that evening. She filled in all the parts she could, interpolating what had happened between Anca and Nancy during the time she was unconscious.

"What did she hit you with?" Ushageeta asked, rubbing macerated herbs into Nancy's shoulder.

Edna answered. "It was a lightning bolt, only very dark, like it sucked all the light out of the room."

"You saw it?" Nancy was able to get the words out.

Edna nodded. "I pretty much saw the whole thing. I could even see Linda's ghost trapped inside the circle."

Ushageeta nodded. "Not all surprising. Binding circles hold spirits in this world, allowing them to be visible by anyone." She frowned at Nancy. "This is going to require some more work. Get me up there," she barked.

Edna and the assistant helped hoist Ushageeta up onto the bed facing Nancy.

"You remember what I did when you first came into my home? I'm going to do something similar. Just hold still. I need to see what this is so I can rout it out."

Ushageeta spread her hands across Nancy's head. This was the third time Nancy had had it done to her in the last twenty-four hours. Her hands were warm to the touch and tingled slightly where they touched Nancy's scalp and forehead.

The sensation was like a sunbeam, warm and inviting.

Then the magic hit and jarred Nancy to her core. She cried out from the shock of it, pushing all the gloom from her mind as this bizarre sensation shot down her spine and into her extremities. Heat and cold intermingled with each other, undulating back and forth, in and out. The braided cord almost felt real, like she could pull on it.

Nancy turned her focus inward. She wasn't sure how she was able to do so, but she suddenly had another type of sight available to her, a sixth sense she'd had all along but wasn't used to using. It felt natural and odd at the same time, like putting on a new set of glasses and being jarred by the sudden clarity, overcome with the newness of it but quickly becoming used to the new, clear sight.

She was floating inside of herself, small and insignificant.

The corded heat and cold retreated, building power inside her.

She turned and saw the blackness, the ever-engulfing darkness that filled her shoulder. It loomed over her like a tidal wave approaching a coastline of unsuspecting tourists. Ushageeta was there, pushing the cord of hot and cold forward, crashing into the expansive wave, like a tiny schooner crashing head-long into a tsunami.

A massive wave crashed. Ushageeta cried out. The cord fell limp.

Nancy jumped in and helped. Like a firefighter holding her hose to fight the blaze, she grabbed the undulating cord and shoved it at the blackness. Together they fought the blackness, driving it back.

A loud crash echoed down the hallway from the kitchen, followed by a wail so gut-wrenching it turned Nancy's stomach.

Ushageeta's assistant screamed.

Nancy and Ushageeta were thrown out of her body. No longer holding onto the cord, they shared a curious glance before turning to look at the door.

Next to the gut-wrenching fear was an internal rumble, a strum on a familiar chord that seemed to balance out the mournful cry. Something was inside her house that she recognized.

Edna jumped. "I'm calling 911!"

Nancy put out her hand to stop Edna. She looked back at Ushageeta. Both women had the same wild-eyed expression.

"Hold that call, Edna. I think I know who it is." Nancy crawled out of bed and crept down the hallway.

Nancy's breaths came slow and careful as she peeked around the foyer into the parlor. A myriad of smells overwhelmed her senses. Charred wood and sweat. Blood and vomit. Decay and death.

Edna sneezed.

"Peter!" Nancy rushed into her parlor where the tiger lay in a heap on the carpet. His sides shook with the labor of breathing. The massive gash in his side oozed blood slowly.

"Get me in there!" Ushageeta snapped at the girl. "Hurry!"

Nancy moved to the side to let Ushageeta through. The frail woman picked herself up by the arms in her wheelchair and barked another order. "Get me down, I need to touch him."

The girl complied, and Nancy jumped in to help maneuver the wheelchair out of the way.

"There, there," Ushageeta cooed to the large, bloody beast lying on the floor. Her voice was soft and tender, a far cry from the barking orders a second before. Nancy wavered between crying and smiling, so happy was she to see him still alive.

"What can I do to help?" Edna, still in the entryway, held a rag to her mouth and danced like a child who needed to go to the bathroom.

Ushageeta turned to her girl. "Get my bag, please." In the same confident, nurturing voice, she turned and gazed at Edna. "Rags. Hot, wet, and sterile."

Edna acknowledged the order with a curt nod. "Got it." She disappeared into the kitchen.

"What about me?" Nancy asked.

Ushageeta leaned over the tiger and opened his eyes. He didn't seem conscious, but was still breathing, though in racking wheezes.

Ushageeta put her thumb on the tiger's forehead, stretching out her fingers over his blood-covered head. The old witch bent and put her ear to the beast's chest, whispering while she did it, so quiet that Nancy barely heard the noise.

Nancy reached out a hesitant hand to touch the fur of the beast. A tear escaped her eye and she frowned. What was she doing? Here was a kid she barely knew, lying bleeding and dying on her pearl-white carpet. If he died, how was she supposed to explain that to anyone? Would Peter change to human form upon death? Her mind raced with a million unanswered questions, none of which she dared entertain for long enough to process the grim reality of what was going on with this young man's life.

She glanced at the witch out of the corner of her eye. She barely knew her, too. Anca had been a horrible person, but Linda seemed like a genuine, good person. Who was Ushageeta? Good? Bad? She'd invited this woman into her house, calling upon some ancient magic that she didn't understand. Anca wanted nothing more than to kill Edna and come live here—

Suddenly a hand rested gently on hers. "Go drink that tea. Ease your mind, then bring me back a cup."

Nancy nodded and stood, her mind a wasteland of emotion. She took a couple steps away then turned, holding on to the doorway for support. "You really are a witch, aren't you?"

Ushageeta, eyes closed as she murmured at the beast again, didn't respond. Nancy tapped the wood with her fingers then asked something else. "Was Anca the bad witch in this town?"

Ushageeta stopped murmuring and turned her head slightly, eyes still on the tiger's chest. "You're not really asking about Anca, are you?"

When Nancy didn't respond, Ushageeta continued. "When you've lived as long as I have with the powers I've been granted, you can't help but have regrets. I would be lying if I said I hadn't done despicable things in my life, possibly worse than what Anca did."

She paused and turned her head more toward Nancy, her face still hidden in profile shadow. "We're all a mix of both, good and bad. Every sentient creature on earth is. But I will do all I can to save this man's life right now, and you have no need to worry for your safety from me."

Nancy smiled as she wiped a tear from her eye then turned and joined Edna in the kitchen.

CHAPTER 23

E DNA WAS BUSY BOILING WATER and handing a tray of steaming terry cloths to Ushageeta's young assistant. Nancy found that the mint, orange peel, and cedar tea was surprisingly good. She felt more energy after drinking it. She washed her hands, grabbed a fresh set of towels from the cupboard and laid them out on the counter for the women to use, and headed back out to give Ushageeta some tea.

All the furniture in Nancy's parlor had been pushed back to the walls.

Ushageeta barked orders and the young attendant ran around the tiger, placing candles and applying sterile cloth to affected areas. Ushageeta was a mess. Her wispy white hair was sweat-soaked and matted to her head. She looked stressed and tired, even though it had only been a few minutes.

Peter's breathing was shallow and erratic.

Nancy handed the steaming cup to the woman, who took the drink and downed the entire thing in one extended gulp.

"That's hot!"

Ushageeta handed the cup back to Nancy. "Not if you do it right." She furrowed her brow. "I didn't finish healing your shoulder." She turned back to the tiger.

Nancy looked at the empty cup in her hand, trying to figure out what had just happened, but decided to worry about it later. She put the cup down on the side table. "I want you to save his life first. How is he doing?"

Ushageeta rubbed her eyes with her hands. "Not good."

Nancy felt her pulse increase, and an unease grew in her stomach. "How bad?"

"Unlike in the movies, therianthropes don't heal better when they are in beast form. Their default state is that of man and they normally only change once a month during a full moon. Anca did something to him, altered his state to force him to be in this form outside of his regular cycle. Because of this, he seems to be stuck and I can't heal him properly. Something is blocking it."

Nancy wrung her hands together. "What can we do?"

Ushageeta looked up at her. "Short of getting a vet? Not sure. I have to get around Anca's lingering magic here, something she's woven deep into him. Normally the shifters keep in packs, so when you turn for the first time, you can imprint on the leader, like a baby duck or wolf imprinting on its mama. I don't think he had this. He didn't have the proper conversion that their kind is used to."

Ushageeta shrugged. "If we had his pack here, or any other were-tiger, they might be able to help him imprint again and get better control over his form. Then they could help him get down off the edge that he's on right now." She paused, studying him. "Hell, I'd even take a werewolf over nothing." She sighed. "But short of that, I have to treat him like a regular tiger even though he's not, and even with that I'm having to fight with whatever Anca's done to him."

Nancy knelt down and brushed her hand across the fur of the tiger before her. "I'm so sorry, Peter. I wish I knew how to help."

Nancy's mind raced. She had come so far, gone through so much, only to have this young man die in her living room, trapped in a furry prison. She hoped to find something, anything that might clue her in to something that could help. A thought popped into her head; it was a long shot. Peter had stolen that book from Anca and given it to her for safekeeping.

"Anca did something to him, something abnormal that you can't get around. What if she had written down the spell in a book?"

Ushageeta furrowed her brow. "Possibly, but I doubt I would have enough time to unravel everything. He's lost a lot of blood and unless I can get him converted back to his default state immediately, I'm stuck."

Nancy stood, her mind whirling. The book had to have the answers Ushageeta needed. Why else would Peter have risked the wrath of Anca to steal it?

"It might have something in there. Let me get it. I can't accept that he's just going to die. Maybe you will know how it works. Maybe it's marked, easy to find."

Nancy crossed her house to the library. The wine bottle sat where she had placed it there the night before, a night that seemed like a distant memory.

She pushed the wine bottle out of the way and opened up the hidden compartment. The space was surprisingly roomy and contained three shelves and a drawer in which to store valuables. The small jade figurine she received from Linda was sitting on the shelf in front of the dark, ancient, leather binding of Anca's spell book. Nancy reached in to move the figurine but stopped. Her hand hovered just above the green mineral. Something about its shape ticked in her brain, the spell runes, etched into its base, called to her from a primal place, a place she had not known existed before this all started, before a witch had died in her arms after being mauled by a were-tiger. Fear, anxiety, and raw power coursed through her spine and down her arms, causing her fingers to tingle and her whole body to shake.

She remembered Linda's words, begging her to return this figurine to Peter, something Nancy had meant to do, but hadn't actually accomplished.

She picked it up, rolling it around, looking at its intricate carvings. The pads of her fingers tingled slightly. This wasn't just an ordinary figurine of a tiger. It had purpose. It had power.

Realization hit Nancy like a six-hundred pound were-tiger.

Giving it back to Peter the first time they met would have simply given it to Anca, same with the second time. Nancy had to ensure that she got Peter away from Anca's clutches before giving it to him. It was the only way to keep Anca from using it against him.

Nancy yelled as she hustled back to Ushageeta. "You said if we had his clan here it would help, right?"

"Yes." Her voice was curt, frustrated.

Nancy was panting as she reentered her living room. "What about something from his pack? What if, when he left to study out of state, they gave him something that would tie themselves to him, so if he turned while he was out of state, he had something to help him through the transition, something to bind him to the pack? Could something like that be put into a small totem?"

"What sort of totem?" Ushageeta's response was hesitant this time, curious.

Nancy chided herself for the casual nature with which she had treated this figurine as she handed it to the old woman.

Ushageeta took the small green tiger and turned it over in her hands. Nancy felt a strange heat emanating from it, even though the other woman held it. Was Ushageeta able to activate it?

Ushageeta looked up at Nancy, tears welling up in her eyes. "Where did you get this?" Her voice wavered and cracked.

The sight of Ushageeta crying flooded Nancy with hope. She was barely able to hold back her own tears. "Linda gave it to me right before she died, asking me to return it to Peter, only I never did. I didn't realize at the time how powerful it was. I … I couldn't feel it until today." Nancy reminded herself that if the figurine had started buzzing with magical energy before the last twenty-four hours, she probably would have brushed it off as some oddity of the stone.

Ushageeta turned over the jade cat again in her fingers.

"Well?" Nancy peered at Ushageeta intently, hoping she would have some miraculous insight into the figurine.

"I don't really know what it does, but it is quite magical. There is great power stored in this. Only, I don't know how to activate it. We would need the person who created it to tell us, or Peter. He was probably instructed in its use before leaving his pack."

Nancy reeled at this information. This was supposed to be the answer! This was supposed to fix him, heal him, make him turn back into a kid she could talk to.

Nothing was going right. Peter was unconscious on her floor. His father was back in California, and Nancy had no idea how to contact him. Everything she knew about magic had been told to her by a ghost.

No, two ghosts; Peter's mother, who had died when Peter was young.

It had to be her figurine. She might have created it. She knew how to unlock it.

And she had told Nancy how.

Nancy held out her hand. "I think I know who made it."

Ushageeta hesitated for a moment, then, narrowing her eyes, finally gave back the figurine. "Anca?"

Nancy shook her head then took a step back. "Peter's mother."

She crawled closer to the tiger. She picked up his right front paw and placed it into her lap. It was heavy and limp and Nancy couldn't help worrying that he was going to wake up any second and attack her. She placed the small figurine on his pads, which dwarfed the tiny statue, and closed the paw around it. She felt the slight twitch of Peter's muscles responding to the stimuli of her hand moving him.

She closed her hands around his paw, squeezing her eyes together. "Please, Peter. Please stay with us. I don't know what else to do to help you, but I hope this is what you need." She thought about Peter's mother, pining to hold her child one last time. Nancy hoped this would work. She needed it to work.

Peter lay motionless in her hands. His breaths so shallow she wondered how any air was getting into his lungs at all. She had been here once before, a bare week ago, holding a dying person's hand while the life slipped away from them. *Do not die on me, Peter! I can't let you die!*

Something welled up inside her, something that had lain dormant all her life. It was white and dark, hot and frigid, furious and caring. It was alive now, coiling around her hand, around his paw, and seeping into the figurine. It would not be contained as the intertwining coil of emotions and magic heated her spine to the boiling point. This was her, this was right. This was her gift, her power, her magic.

She looked down at the tiger, but she saw through him to the boy underneath. The blue-white glow of his spirit lay limp on the ground.

She continued to allow the flow of energy to course through her body, down her arms, and into the statue, which seemed to gobble up everything she poured into it.

A hum emanated from Peter's paw, followed by a cold, sapphire light. Nancy hugged his paw harder, closing her eyes and concentrating on Peter and his pain. She willed him with everything she could mentally throw at him, to get better, to respond somehow, to come back so that she could tell him what Linda's dying wish had been. So she could tell him his mother loved him.

She felt … something. Another cord. Another entity in the statue. Nancy pulled and the entity slid easily out, a blue spirit that was instantly recognizable to her. It was Peter's mother from the dream she'd had only a day before.

She was young and thin, with hair down to her waist. The two locked eyes for only a moment before the woman turned and gazed down on her son.

The ghost knelt and picked up Peter's spirit's head. She placed it in her lap and stroked his cheek, pushing the long, matted hair away from his face. Her expression was as solemn as a stone as she took in his now fully-grown look.

Then Peter's mother began to cry.

CHAPTER 24

P ETER GROWLED. A HEAT ENVELOPING him, starting
at his paw holding the figurine and traveling all over his body,
light following the warmth. Over a few seconds, Nancy felt
the massive paw shrink, fur retracting, disappearing, until she was
holding onto the smooth, clammy skin of a young man.

The ghostly spirit of Peter's mother was gone.

Peter groaned. Nancy opened her eyes, then immediately
turned her head when she realized he was fully naked. Nancy
felt herself go red.

From behind them, Edna snickered.

Ushageeta smiled.

Nancy looked up at the old woman carefully. "I didn't think
he would be naked."

"Did you think he would be wearing shorts?"

Nancy shrugged. "Guess I didn't think about it. This is all so
new to me."

Ushageeta sighed. "Yes. And you and I have some things
to discuss, but not now. Now that he's human again, I can start
working on the damage." She furrowed her brow at Nancy. "We
need to discuss your shoulder, too, don't forget. And I want to
know how you were able to be in there with me."

"I know, but spend your energy on him, please. I'm okay."
Despite that, Nancy could still sense the darkness inside
herself. They had not had time to push it back fully before
being interrupted.

Nancy chanced a look at him, just because he had changed form did not take away the injuries he had sustained. If anything, they looked significantly worse on his stark light skin and much smaller body than they had on his large tiger frame.

Nancy got up and retrieved a sheet to cover him and a blanket to replace the warmth that he had just been getting from the fur. Ushageeta grabbed more herbs out of her satchel.

An hour later, Ushageeta gave the okay for Nancy to come back.

Peter was propped up slightly, pillows under him as he lay on the couch and smiled weakly at her as she came in.

"Ma'am," he said after she adjusted his blanket and set a cup of hot tea on the table beside him.

She smiled. "Good to see you." She brushed back his unruly hair.

He still held onto the small jade figurine in his hand. Nancy smiled. "I'm glad you are doing better."

She glanced at Ushageeta, now sitting in her wheelchair again. Ushageeta gave her the slightest of nods, calming her fears, assuring her that Peter would be okay.

"You two talk. I need to go make a phone call to Peter's father."

She left the room, leaving Nancy and Peter alone.

CHAPTER 25

I'M AMAZED THAT YOU HEALED so well." Nancy thought about putting out her hand to touch his barely-scarred side. It seemed unreal.

Peter ran his hand over his side. "I don't remember what happened."

Nancy sat down on the couch beside him, holding her own cup of tea close to her nose so she could inhale the aroma. "It's probably best that you don't. It was … unpleasant."

He looked up at her, lip quivering. Nancy finally felt compelled to put an arm around him and give him a great big hug. She settled for a light touch on his shoulder.

"What she made you do while in that state is not your fault."

He looked up at her, eyes moist. "I know. I just feel terrible for everything going on."

Nancy put on her stern face. "You were the victim here. You and Linda, of Anca and her evil plans. I don't want you to forget that. She was the one that forced you to do things against your will. That is a violation. Her. Not you."

He smiled, a weak, almost shy smile, but it warmed Nancy's heart to know that he could smile after all of that.

"Thank you."

"You call me if you ever need reminding."

They sat in a comfortable silence for a moment, sipping their tea. Nancy finally broke the silence.

"I don't know if you want to talk about it, but while you are … well, a tiger … how does it feel?"

Peter sloshed his tea around in contemplation, or avoidance—Nancy wasn't sure which—but he finally responded. "I don't remember. Honestly. It's a bit of a haze." He looked up at her eyes to drive the point. "Have you ever been so angry at someone or something that you could not see other things around you? You just have that one thing that you cannot see around. So focused that you ignore your safety and all rational thought?"

Nancy's mind drifted to her husband. Their entire married life had been relatively argument-free but she could remember, long ago, a couple intense fights and the single-minded rage she held in her mind during those times. Of course she knew; it was a shared human condition.

"It's like that," Peter continued, jerking his hand slightly to punctuate the point. Nancy saw the tea slosh out of his cup slightly, a drip going down the outside of the cup and onto his knee. "I can't remember anything, really, just this red rage clouding my mind. I do have fleeting single images, though."

"Did you know what was going on with the whole tiger thing?"

He shook his head, glancing back down at the figurine. "My father gave me this the day I left for college. He pulled me off to the side with my uncle. I remember that day because my father and his brother rarely talk. Things have always been strained between the two of them, but that day they were both there, talking to me in hushed tones, sharing looks.

"He told me that he loved me. It was the first time in my life he ever said that, but he gave me the totem and said to call him if I ever got any funny feelings or something.

"I remember laughing and telling him I already went through puberty and I already had those feelings, but my uncle chimed in and told him to just tell me. Then my dad shot him a look and I swear, he growled. At the time, I didn't think anything of it, but thinking back, I see what that meeting was all about. Anyway, he told me again to keep the figurine close, keep it with me at all times and, and to call him if something strange happens."

He turned the figurine over a couple times in his hand and looked back up at her. "I guess this counts as strange, huh?"

Nancy laughed. It felt good, cathartic.

The last week had been a tumult of excitement and she was not one used to such excitement in her life.

A shuffle and squeak behind her made Nancy turn around. Ushageeta came into the room, pushed by her assistant.

"I spoke to your father," she said as the young woman came to a stop with the wheelchair.

"How much does he know?"

"Enough. There were a lot of details that are hard to really place given your … odd … change over. Normally you have the benefit of a pack to help you navigate the rough waters of this time in your life. You haven't had that. He asked me to get you a plane ticket to head back home."

"Plane flight?" Nancy asked.

"He needs to get back to see his family. That figurine, no matter how powerful and personal, was meant as a stopgap measure till he can return to his pack. He needs them to recover from all of this."

Peter nodded. "What about my studies?"

"Those will need to be put on hold for a while, but don't worry." Ushageeta gave an odd, toothy smile. Nancy had seen her smile before, but only while making fun of Edna. This was different. "I think this is a little more important."

Nancy hesitated before turning to Ushageeta. "I want to thank you for your help, for coming over here."

Ushageeta reached out and placed her hand on Nancy's. "I am just glad he's alive. Plus, you did the real magic, young lady."

"I have questions." Nancy had avoided thinking about what had happened. The whole situation was too surreal. She needed to have some closure with Peter before she could worry about herself. Her shoulder still hurt like hell every time she moved it.

Ushageeta squeezed Nancy's hand. "I'm sure you do, but those will need to wait until this matter is put behind us. I still stand by what I told you at my house yesterday. You are meddling with dangerous things here. You need to be careful and cautious, not curious. Everything that happened last night was because you put your nose where it didn't belong."

Nancy opened her mouth to defend her actions, but Ushageeta raised her hand to signal silence. "I understand, I really do. But it doesn't change the truth. You have questions, but I cannot promise I have answers. I will help where I can, but there are things that you simply cannot know for now. I know it's a horrible answer, but that's what I can offer. For now, get some sleep and get that boy to the airport. I will head home, if that is okay with you."

Nancy nodded. "Thank you."

Ushageeta nodded curtly while calling for her assistant.

Nancy turned to Edna, who had been sitting back watching everyone. Nancy felt bad seeing her best friend sitting on the periphery of the action.

"Thank you for pulling me out of that building. I wasn't myself."

Edna gave her a big bear hug. "You would have done the same for me."

Nancy fought back a tear. "I'm sorry for putting you in so much danger. I should have never let Anca in and I should have run when Linda told me so."

Edna released the hug and held Nancy at arm's length. "Now you listen here, girl. We have been through a lot and I have barreled blindly into situations I shouldn't, but you were always there to back me up. I'm the one hell-bent on living life to the fullest, remember? You have nothing to be ashamed of. Peter is alive and free from Anca's grasp. We're all okay."

Nancy's throbbing shoulder reminded her that not everything was okay, but Edna did have a point. Still, Nancy needed to learn so much about these new powers so she didn't put her friends in harm's way again.

"Thank you." It was all she could muster. She barely kept her emotions in check.

"And my best friend is a witch! How cool is that?" Edna's eyes sparkled like a kid in a candy store. "Now I'm going to get out of here. I could really use my own bed. I think I'll be sleeping for a couple days, given how crazy the last few were. Call you when I wake up?"

The next morning Nancy stood at the entrance to the terminal. She hugged Peter and bade him a good and safe trip.

"Call me when you land and let me know when you plan on coming back. You are always welcome to stay with me."

"Thank you." Peter turned and started up the ramp, then stopped and turned back.

"That book," he said in hushed tones.

Nancy tensed. "What about it?"

"It dangerous. I don't think I have to tell you about that, but I felt like I needed to say it."

She smiled. "Of course it is. I have Ushageeta at hand to help me with it."

Peter smiled then rolled the tips of his fingers together in what seemed like serious contemplation.

"What is it?" Nancy inquired.

"I don't think you should tell Ushageeta about it, at least not yet. Anca got that book from someone in, well, I don't know who he is, but Anca was terrified of him. She borrowed it, but he's been asking for it back and she refused. Right now the only ones who know you have it are us. If word got out that you had it, he would hunt you down."

Nancy nodded. "I'll be careful, I promise."

"Oh and speaking of the book. Behind that secret door you said no one else knew about?"

"Yes."

"I left you something that might be the key to opening the book. I didn't want to tell you before, but now, with Anca ..." He glanced at the security lines as if making sure no one was eavesdropping. "I didn't think it was safe enough to leave with the book. But please be careful. I don't think it should be opened."

Nancy put her hand on his shoulder and smiled warmly. "You will be late. Go see your family."

After stopping by the diner for a quick breakfast, Nancy arrived back at her home a little over an hour after watching Peter's plane take off.

Her house felt larger and emptier. She thought about how much had changed in just one week.

She stood in the parlor for a time before running her hand over the arm of one of her Queen Anne chairs. If anything, they seemed cleaner than she had kept them. Ushageeta did not tell her how she had made all the blood disappear, and Nancy did not really want to know.

She thought about the key upstairs and toyed with going to find it, but stopped herself just as her hand rested on the baluster of her stairs. No, the key would wait. Despite her incessant curiosity, she would heed the advice of her elders, or youngsters in this matter. Prudence seemed to be the name of the game here.

That should have put Nancy's mind at ease, but it didn't, at least not fully. If that book was as dangerous as everyone kept telling her, it might be best to just leave it hidden.

She began to brew some tea and grabbed the copy of *The Notebook* Richard had been reading. She sat down in the library facing the empty fireplace.

She barely made it through the first chapter before she fell asleep, dreaming of faeries flittering around her shoulder.

EPILOGUE

DRAGON LOOKED UP AT THE knock on his office door. "Martin, come in, I was just looking at something."

"What is it, boss?"

Dragon spun the piece of paper around and showed him a picture of a couple of women in a crowd.

"Do you recognize these two, Martin?"

"Uh yes, boss, I do. We spoke to them in the car a while back."

"That's right, and afterward I asked you to track them down."

"We did, but we lost them, sir." He was nervous. Dragon understood that nervousness, and smiled to help calm the dumb troll's nerves.

"That's quite alright there, Martin, quite alright. We have a small problem and a big problem on our hands now, though."

"What is the small problem?"

Dragon produced another picture, taken from the same location in the city, of a burning building, completely engulfed in flames with a large crowd huddled around it.

"That's the building! I was there."

"Yes, you were, Martin. Yes, you were, and while you and your idiot brother failed to notice the two women we met in the street a few nights ago, I had someone else taking pictures, so at least we know what they look like and we can start looking around for them. There aren't *that* many witches in this town. We should be able to make it well known that we are very interested in finding out who they are."

"Uh, boss, you said there was a bigger problem?"

"The bigger problem is this." He tapped the picture of the building in flames. "We've been all over the wreckage and we can't find the book."

"The book?"

"Yes, I know you know what book I'm talking about, because that book used to sit right over there."

Dragon pointed to the corner with a long, bony arm.

On the top of the slanted wooden stand was a large rectangular portion that stood out, lacking the sheen that the rest of the stand, particularly the sides, had.

"We need that book back. Will you help me find it?"

"Yes, boss, of course."

Dragon nodded a moment, eying his subordinate up and down. "We also have an even bigger problem."

Martin shifted in his seat. "What's that?"

"We didn't find Anca's or the theran's remains. I want you to keep an eye out, you hear me?"

Martin nodded, a stricken look on his face.

"Good, Martin. Now go eat some food. You will feel happier once you have eaten."

Dragon sighed as soon as the door closed. He leaned back in his chair as far as it would allow him and ran his fingers through his hair. Martin was dumb, but loyal. The other one he wasn't so sure about. He preferred loyalty to brains, but the two were inseparable.

He got up, stretching his back. He hated sitting at desks. He was not cut out for this life, pushing paper and keeping appointments. What use was sitting down when you could accomplish so much more standing up?

He walked around his desk, thumping the empty spot twice with his knuckles where the *Book of Endless Shadow* once lay. He would get it back, that wasn't a concern at this point. He just hoped he would obtain it before the Tael made their annual visit.

He locked his door then jiggled the handle to ensure it was truly secure.

He added a magical lock for good measure and turned around to the wall behind his desk.

A wave of his hand caused a doorway to materialize in front of him, nearly as wide as his desk. The darkness on the other side of the threshold sucked in the light from the office, causing it to vanish into the depths.

Dragon took a step into the room beyond before stopping, removing his coat, and rolling up his sleeves. No sense them getting dirty.

As he placed the coat on the back of his chair, he heard a whimper from behind.

He turned around and cracked his knuckles. The popping sound echoing off the stone walls in the inky blackness. A rustle in the darkness, a slight movement. The sound of metal on metal clinking. It was all music to his ears.

In the distance, he could just barely make out the hunched over disfigured form of a human. He smiled and took a step into the darkness, waiting for his eyes to adjust.

The form took more shape, allowing him to see the cuts on the skin and the blistery burns all around. The figure huddled in the corner, naked, hairless, shaking.

The room was cold, too cold for comfort, but Dragon didn't mind. In just a minute, it would be quite warm.

He took a few more steps in, hands off to the side, glowing with red heat. "I miss these little meetings of ours. You ready to feel the burn?"

AFTERWORD

Thank you for taking a chance on me! I know there are a lot of us out there, an endless sea of self-published authors, and you chose me.

As a thank you, I wrote a short story that sheds light on the backstory of Linda and Anca, and I would like to give it to you. This story is not available for purchase, as I only want to share it with those who loved *A Moonlit Task*.

Sign up for my newsletter. Visit www.scarhoof.com/splashes to sign up and I will send you the free short story "Splashes of Wine". If you wish to know about any of my upcoming works, please consider signing up to my mailing list. I will always respect your privacy and you can unsubscribe at any time with one click.

Did you leave a review on Amazon or Goodreads? If so, tell me about it! Contact info is on my About the Author page at the end of the book, or email me scarhoofwrites@gmail.com.

I love reading reviews of my books and you will have my eternal gratitude! Reviews help new authors like myself be found by other readers.

Thank you so much for your support! I'm already hard at work for the next book in Nancy's story and I can't wait to share it with you!

About A Moonlit Task

"Red for the Chevy, Yellow for the shop," Linda Hamada muttered to herself as she stepped from her tiny herb shop into the alleyway.

The original opening for this book's first draft changed significantly since I wrote those first words.

Nancy Moon originally began as a thought experiment: What would Nancy Drew be like as a Grandmother? I didn't know what a Cozy Mystery was back then, I just thought it might be cool to have an older protagonist. I normally read fantasy, and too often it's a young farm boy that gets swept up in some epic plot. Lately it's barely been about young kick-ass women in their 20's that seem to have all the skills of the latest Hollywood action movie. I wanted something different, something unique.

I wrote the first version of *A Moonlit Task* in 2014 for NaNoWriMo, a worldwide yearly movement for authors to write a novel in one month. I completed the minimum 50,000 words in the month of November, and went on to complete the manuscript in December of that year.

I put the story away for a month or two, and pulled it back out early in 2015. By then I had spent months critiquing other people's stories from my writing group, and I also had done a beta read for one member's book. Those hours spent critiquing other people's writing allowed me to begin seeing the mistakes I was making in my own writing. I had grown quite a bit since I had first came up with the outline for this book, and looking at my raw manuscript again I knew I could do better.

Starting in March of 2015, I re-wrote this book from scratch. Once completed, I began the arduous process of editing. I submitted a few chapters to my writing group and went through the entire manuscript by myself, cutting scenes, and adding new ones. Taking feedback and consulting my original draft to see what I did differently and in the end I combined my favorite part of both drafts to create my finished manuscript.

That took almost a year, off and on. Time for beta readers.

Spring of 2016 I sent off a call to friends, family, and co-workers to get beta readers. Thirty generous souls agreed to read my mess of a book. Two months later, I received an overwhelming amount of feedback and would need a lot of time to get through it all. I started sifting. All summer long I worked and worked, refining my story based on the feedback.

I then sent the book off to a copy editor to correct grammar and punctuation and began working on cover designs. The first concept blew me away. After a little back and forth, we found the perfect model and after only three revisions, we had the final cover.

That is how Nancy went from my head to yours. It's been a couple years now, which I have to say, isn't too bad, especially for my first book. I'm already working on the next book in the series so we will definitely be seeing Nancy and Edna real soon.

I hope you enjoy this story. It's very dear to my heart. An unlikely hero, Nancy represents the pent up demand for someone older than their twenties to save the world. This is not your Grandmother's Cozy Mystery. Buckle up because Nancy's world is going to get turned upside down.

-Tom Hansen
February 2017

ACKNOWLEDGMENTS

Publishing a book is not a solo affair. I had to come up with the concept, write the outline, and put in the work to write and edit. But that's only a small part of the process. So many people helped with this book coming to market.

I have to give thanks:

To my dear wife: Jennifer. You loved this story from the first concept and have been a constant cheerleader for Nancy, Edna, and me. The only reason I didn't give up was because I knew how much you wanted this story to come out.

To my writing group: Aeon, Amber, DeAnna, Lisa, and Tara. Your bi-weekly feedback and sage advice took me from being a wanna-be to a will-be. You are the reason I'm an author and not a writer. You helped me navigate the tricky waters of writing Nancy as a believable woman. I couldn't have done it without you!

To my Beta Readers: all twenty of you. I received way more feedback than I originally thought I would have to go through, but this book is significantly better for it. My antagonist was a megalomaniac Bond villain before you helped me. You found endless typos, blocking issues, and inconsistencies. It was a lot of work fixing everything but I couldn't have done it without your feedback.

To my Copy Editor: Claire. You are a lifesaver. You made me not look like a fool with horrible grammar and punctuation, but you also did it in an unbelievable short amount of time. You even edited your own acknowledgement!

To my Cover Designer: Deranged Doctor Designs. Your first cover concept looked like a work of art and after only three revisions and a little hunting around for just the right model for my concept of Nancy, we had it. You guys do amazing work and have bent over backwards for me to work around my timeline in order to get this book out the door.

To everyone else: Various friends, family members, authors, and the writing communities that I trolled over the last six years have given me the knowledge, confidence, and gumption to plow forward into the scary world of self publishing.

To my readers: You are taking a chance on an unknown author. I hope I do not let you down.

-Tom Hansen
February 2017

ABOUT THE AUTHOR

Tom Hansen lives in Arizona with his lovely wife, four teenage children, and two cats. Systems Engineer by day, and writer by night, he also finds time to run a gaming channel on YouTube.

A Moonlit Task is his first published novel and he has many more stories left in his aging noggin to release to the world.

Visit him at his website www.scarhoof.com to learn more about him and his upcoming projects!